RIDIN' DIRTY WITH A DOWN SOUTH MILLIONAIRE 3

DEJAH RICE

Cole Hart

Ridin' Dirty With A Down South Millionaire 3

Copyright © 2021 by Dejah Rice

All rights reserved.

Published in the United States of America.

Mailing List

To stay up to date on new releases, plus get information on contests, sneak peeks, and more,

Go To The Website Below...

www.colehartsignature.com

A NOTE FROM BISHOP

I was always told that a woman would be my biggest downfall, and I believed it for the longest... until I met a woman who wasn't like anyone I'd ever met before. She was the change I needed, or at least that was what I was led to believe. But these bitches were no different than being out in the streets. I always had to watch my back with them, or they would one up me when I least expected it.

Luckily, I was always ten steps ahead, and I learned that just because someone was in your car, it didn't mean they were riding for you. The beginning might've been the end, but the end was the beginning, and this last ride was about to go fast.

RAHEEM

"Oh hell no! I'm calling my brother!" Brandy said, turning on her heels, and I jumped up from the bed.

"Brandy, wait!" I yelled as I followed her out the door.

"What the fuck is wrong with you, Rah? Why would you go and do some shit like that? Seriously? You know what Bishop has been through, and you go and shove your tongue down his wife's throat? What the hell is going on between the two of you? And I want the truth." She crossed her arms over her chest and looked me up down with a stern expression on her face.

"Sis, chill and let me explain." I held my hands up, but she was quick to cut me short.

"We're all family, but shit hasn't been right between you and Bishop since Munchie entered the picture. She's turned shit upside down for y'all, and I know she's been through a lot, but that's no excuse for this shit right here. I looked at her like my little sister and sympathized with the low-down bitch!" she yelled loud like she wanted to make sure Munchie could hear her as we stood right outside the door.

"What about yo' fucking brother!" Munchie yelled, and I heard BJ start to cry.

"What is she talking about? Because I'm real close to whooping her fucking ass." Brandy bobbed her head up and down and started taking her earrings out. I reached behind me and closed the door. I could hear Munchie yelling something, but I didn't bother to see what it was.

"Look, Brandy, it's a lot of shit goin' on that you don't know about."

"Obviously." She tilted her head to the side.

"Can we go downstairs and talk?" I asked, but she didn't respond right away.

She looked at me, and I could tell the wheels were spinning in her head. Brandy had never been dumb, but the last thing I needed was for her to figure out the truth. Being caught kissing Munchie was one thing, but being the father of her baby was something completely different. The kiss was fixable, but it wasn't no turning back once anyone found out about our child. I didn't know how I was going to get out of the shit, but I'd promised Munchie I had us, and I meant that.

"No. Once I go back downstairs, I don't ever want to see your ass again. You have two minutes to tell me what the fuck is going on." She tapped her high heel rapidly.

"Bishop and Munchie have been going through a lot. Bishop had a baby on Munchie, but I guess you didn't know that." I looked down the hallway as a nurse walked by.

"Wait a minute. What?" she asked, touching her temple like she was trying to process what I'd just said.

"It ain't my place to tell you this shit, but Bishop had a daughter a few days after Munchie was released from prison. Her name is Bella, and she's nine months old. So Munchie ain't been herself. She was venting to me about her problems, and out of impulse, I kissed her. It was wrong, and I can admit that shit."

"Oh, God," she sighed, shaking her head. "And I thought I was the only one going through shit, but at least I managed to pull myself back together. I don't know what the fuck the three of you are going to do, but I don't want no parts of this shit.

Y'all have made a big-enough mess on your own. Bishop having babies on Munchie. Munchie kissing you behind his back. Have all of you lost your fucking minds!" she yelled.

"Ay, chill." I attempted to shush her.

"Don't tell me to fucking chill!"

"You right. My bad, but what you want me to say, Brandy? I fucked up, but that shit won't happen again. I can promise you that. I just felt bad for her. That's all. Do me a favor please?" I cocked my head to the side.

"What the hell is it?"

"Don't tell Bishop."

"Are you fucking crazy?" she asked, but I could tell her mind wandered off because she got real silent after that.

She'd just said she was staying out of it, and now she was backtracking. My damn hands were sweaty, and my back was starting to itch from the anticipation. If she told Bishop about the kiss, that was going to lead to a hell of a lot more problems. Problems that I didn't need but problems I'd caused at the same damn time. She was right; we'd made a mess out of an already fucked-up situation. Munchie could've fucked anyone behind Bishop's back, but it just had to be me.

The fucked-up part was, I'd been the one who initiated the shit. But no one couldn't convince me that Munchie didn't come over for that exact reason. Her eyes told on her from the moment she walked on my porch. I didn't have to follow up on the shit, but I didn't expect to fall in love with Munchie either. The deed was already done though and all I could do now was find a fucking way out.

"Brandy," I said after she never responded.

"I'm not goin' to tell him."

"Thank you, sis—" I started to say before she cut me off by holding her hand up in the air.

"Ain't no 'sis' nothing." She pointed her long nail in my face. "I'm not keeping it to myself for your or Munchie's ass. I'm doin' it for my brother because I don't want him to end up in prison for the rest of his life like our father for killing you grimy motherfuckers! Lord have mercy on your souls." She walked away after looking me up and down, and my thoughts immediately went to Bishop.

One of us was a dead man walking, and it sure as hell wasn't me.

2

BISHOP

"Fine, I guess you'll see your daughter whenever," she said and then grabbed her suitcase and walked past me.

"Nah, bitch. You gon' see my daughter whenever," I said and then eased my gun out of my waistband before pulling the trigger right as she turned around. **Pow!**

She fell to the floor, holding on to her chest and looking at me with tear-filled eyes like she couldn't believe I'd shot her. I walked over and squatted down next to her as I shook my head. She'd brought this shit on herself. She'd practically been asking for it, and I'd given her what she'd been looking for. I didn't repeat myself often, and I sure as hell didn't give no warnings, but she had both and still wanted to fuck with me.

"What about our daughter?" she struggled to ask.

"That's for me to figure out. All you ever had to do was stay in yo' fuckin' place, but you couldn't do that. I'll see you in hell, bitch," I said and then walked out as her eyes closed.

Once I was outside, I looked around to make sure no one was around, and then I took off running to my car. When I got inside, I started it up and sped away from the crime scene. My mind raced as I drove down the street. I looked in the rearview mirror, and I almost wrecked the damn car when I saw my father's face instead of mine.

I shook that shit out my head quick. I was nothing like that nigga. I had a reason to do what I did. She wanted to take my child away from me, and I couldn't allow it. I wanted to feel bad, but I didn't.

Matter fact, I wasn't feeling shit but numbness. I knew where I could go to get my mind off shit though, and twenty minutes later, I pulled up to the strip club in the middle of the day. I parked my car and took the hoodie I was wearing off. Once I tossed it in the passenger's seat, I jumped out the car and headed inside. I found a seat in the cut and sat there for about ten minutes before a bartender finally strutted over to me.

"Can I get you something to drink, Bishop?" she questioned, and I wasn't surprised she knew my name. Everybody around the city knew who the fuck I was.

"It's 'bout damn time! I been sitting here for damn near an hour," I snapped. I played shit just right so I would have the perfect alibi if it ever came to that.

"Really? I apologize, but it's hard to see you sitting over here," she said and then licked her juicy, pink lips that matched the pink wig on her head. "Why didn't you come over to the bar?" she questioned, and I looked at her sideways.

"Do I look like a peasant ass nigga to you? I don't come to workers; workers come to me," I said, and she laughed like I was a comedian.

"You so silly."

"Fuck all that. Get me some Patrón on the rocks." I waved her off, and she popped her tongue.

"I got you." She walked away and strutted extra hard, but I didn't trip off her voluptuous ass.

When I felt my phone vibrate in my pocket, I pulled it out and saw it was a text from Brandy that said she couldn't make it, because one of her kids had gotten sick. I didn't even bother to respond, because I was used to Brandy fucking with me whenever she chose to. It wasn't no big deal, and I wasn't in the mood to go back to the hospital right then anyway.

"Here you go." A mixed-looking chick approached the table with my drink.

"Don't I know you?" I questioned as she placed my drink down. She looked at me like she recognized me too, and then she snapped her fingers.

"You know what? I do recognize you. I was at your baby shower from hell." She laughed, and I instantly knew where I'd seen her before. She was Raheem's girl, and they'd walked into the baby shower right before Rissa's dumb ass came in on some bullshit. Luckily, I wouldn't have those problems anymore.

"That's right."

"Yes, you're Munchie's husband!" she yelled excitedly.

"I am. You know my wife?" I grabbed my glass and took a few sips.

"I'm Dula. I was locked up with her." She smiled.

"Word? Yeah, I remember her telling me 'bout you. How da fuck you get involved wit' Raheem?"

"We met here actually, but we're not together anymore. That muthafucka broke up wit' me." She twisted her face up, and I could tell she got pissed at just the thought of it.

What I found strange was that Raheem had been acting like he still had a girlfriend. I didn't know if he dumped shawty for somebody else or what. But the nigga had most definitely blew me off repeatedly to chill with some bitch. Then again, it was Rah, so I wasn't even surprised. He couldn't settle down if somebody paid him to do that shit.

"Oh, damn. I ain't know," I said, tossing the rest of my drink back and then slamming the cup down. "Lemme get another one," I demanded.

"Okay. Do you mind if I join you? I would really like to hear how Munchie is doing," she said, and I looked at her for a second. I really wanted to be left alone, but if I talked to her, it would be the perfect distraction from my thoughts.

"You not working?"

"Nah. I come in early to clean the bathrooms and help the bartender do a stock check, cut up fruit to go in the drinks, and shit like that. But she got it," she informed me, and I nodded.

"Cool." I watched her as she walked away and went back over to the bar. She was dressed down with her hair in a ponytail, and I figured she would get ready for the night later on. It wasn't too many people inside, and I guess that was why they still opened early to get shit ready for the night. While shawty got my drink, my phone vibrated again, and when I looked at it, I saw Rissa's mama's name on the screen. I took a deep breath before I answered the call. "What's up?" I questioned, and I wasn't surprised at all when I heard her scream and cry through the phone.

"Bishop! I need you to come get Bella now. Rissa's best friend, Ari, just called me and told me she found Rissa shot in her home. They're rushing her to the hospital!" she yelled, and everything went silent. That bitch was still alive.

3

BABY JO

"Watch out," Stunna said and pushed me to the floor as T-Bank pulled the trigger.

Pow! Pow! He shot Stunna twice, and Stunna's body slapped the ground. Ajay screamed at the top of her lungs and ran over to where her daddy was.

"Get my daughter and let's go. Now!" T-Bank yelled and turned the gun on me. I quickly went and snatched Sunny up. "Now let's fucking go and don't try shit or yo' ass is next," he said as he pulled the door open and waited for me to walk out.

"Daddy, get up! Daddy!" Ajay yelled and tried to shake Stunna. Then she looked up at me as I neared the door. "Please don't leave us. I'm scared," she cried as T-Bank forced Sunny and me out the door.

I watched as he closed the door behind him, and all I could focus on was the gun in his hand. I had to get that shit away from him and quick. My life literally depended on it, and so did my daughter's. The only reason I ever agreed to come with him was because I didn't want anyone to get hurt. It was too late for that though, and if I didn't do something quick, Stunna would bleed out on my damn living room floor. I couldn't allow that to happen, and I felt like shit for even putting him and his daughter in such a situation. I just knew if he made it out alive, he would hate me forever, but I had to do something.

"Sunny, can you walk, baby?" I asked, and she nodded, so I placed her down on the ground.

"What da fuck you putting her down for? Pick her ass up and get to da car," T-Bank growled. "I swear fo' God if you keep playin' wit', me I'ma splatter yo' shit right now," he threatened.

"You don't even have a car seat for her. Don't do this shit. Leave while you can and don't look back," I begged.

"Bitch, let's go." He picked Sunny up, and I had no choice but to follow him to his car. He opened the back door and put Sunny inside before he pulled the seat belt over her body. Once she was secured, he looked at me over the top of the car. "Get da fuck in!" he yelled, and I tried to get in the back with Sunny. "In da front so I can see yo' trifling ass." I reluctantly closed the back door and got inside on the passenger's side while he got in the car as well and slammed his door shut.

"How did you find me?" I asked right when he was about to stick the key in the ignition. The gun sat on his lap, and I made sure not to pay it too much attention.

"I sent my mama down here to find yo' stupid ass. She went to yo' mama's church and followed her from there until eventually she led her here. I been had the address," he bragged, and the fact that he talked to me instead of pulling off told me everything I needed to know. He was high out of his mind and allowed his emotions to run him instead of his brain. That told me I still had a chance. I just had to keep him talking.

"So you been knowing where I was and just now decided to come? You don't care about us."

"No, bitch! You da one who don't give a fuck. You think I don't know Bishop and Raheem would've been on my ass if I pulled up at the wrong time, huh?"

"No. You found out I was moving on somehow and decided to ruin that for me like you ruin everything else."

"You ain't seen shit yet. And it wasn't hard to figure out. My cousin told me all about you posting pictures wit' this nigga on ya Instagram, so you damn right I had to come put a stop to that shit. You a trifling bitch, and you ain't never been shit and won't ever be shit but a dick-sucking hoe! Don't forget I know you better than you know yo'self. That nigga don't want shit from you but ya pussy. But you always have been good at making money off that shit." He smirked, and I lost it.

Wap! I punched him in the side of the face as hard as I could, and his head hit the window. I didn't hesitate to grab the gun off his lap, and then I started to beat his ass with it. I guess he'd forgotten who the fuck I was, but when it came to throwing hands with the nigga, I was never scared. That fear had left my body years ago, and with my daughter in the back seat, my emotions had tripled.

"You can't have me or my fuckin' daughter!" I yelled and continued my assault. I was damn near in his seat with him as I went crazy, and Sunny started screaming in the back.

"Have you lost yo' fuckin' mind!" T-Bank yelled as he pushed me off him, and I flew back into my own seat. Before he could do anything else, I upped the gun and pulled the trigger. **Pow!** I opened my door and jumped out the car before snatching the back door open.

"Sunny, come to mommy," I said in a panicked tone, and she crawled across the seat to me. I grabbed her up in my arms and ran back to my condo as fast as I could.

Once I got inside, I locked my door and placed Sunny down. Then I found my phone and dialed 911 immediately. After I told them my emergency and gave them my address, I put the phone on speaker and placed it on the couch since the dispatcher told me not to hang up. I quickly grabbed Ajay and Sunny and took them to Sunny's bedroom, and right before I walked out, Ajay stopped me.

"Miss. Jody, is my daddy going to be okay?" she asked, wrapping her arms around me, and a tear rolled down my cheek as I reached down to rub her back.

"I hope so, sweetie," I said, unable to lie to her. "Y'all stay in here for me, okay?" I asked, and she nodded. I walked out the room and pulled the door closed. They had seen enough, and I knew the situation we were in would probably traumatize them for life. But I prayed they would be able to forget it one day. I ran back to the living room and dropped to my knees beside Stunna. "Hold on, baby. Help is on the way. You can't leave me like this. Please, Stunna, fight for your daughter," I cried as someone started to bang on the door. I didn't know if it was T-Bank or the police. **Boom! Boom! Boom!**

❧ 4 ❧

MUNCHIE
A FEW DAYS LATER

"**A**lrighty, Mrs. King. It looks like you're almost all set to go. The doctor will be in with your discharge papers shortly. Congratulations on your bundle of joy and let me know if you need anything before you leave."

"Thanks, Cathy," I said as the nurse walked out of my room.

She was an older woman with a little weight on her, and she reminded me of somebody's auntie. The one who would look out for you but wouldn't play no games though. She was always on top of things her whole shift, and she made sure everyone did what they were supposed to do when it came to me, which was appreciated because I had a few nurses I wanted to slap the fuck out of during my stay just because their attitudes were nasty. It was obvious they were in the field for the the money and not the actual damn job.

Bishop was supposed to go downstairs and pull the car around to the front, but he'd forgotten the damn car seat, so he was gone to get that while I sat in my room with Baby Jo. I was on the edge of the bed rocking BJ in my arms while she sat on the couch and bounced her legs up and down. The last few days hadn't been easy for her at all, and I was worried about her.

"Baby Jo," I said, and she didn't answer me right away, so I called her again. "Jody."

"Huh?" she asked, looking up at me with bloodshot eyes.

I could tell she hadn't slept much, and her hair was pulled up into a messy bun. She had on sweats, and she wasn't wearing any makeup. That wasn't like her at all, because Jody took pride in keeping her appearance up. Even when she was on drugs, she made sure to be on point at all times. That was how I knew things were taking a toll on her, and I wished I could help.

"You good?"

"Girl, no, but I'll be alright. My nerves are just shot." She shook her head.

"I can understand that. How's Stunna doing?" I questioned since he was at the same hospital.

I couldn't believe the shit T-Bank pulled. It had damn near been three years, and he was still on the same crap. It didn't make any sense, and it had me mad as hell that he would come back right when she was starting to move on. She deserved to be happy, and he didn't have the right to take that away from her. I was just glad that Jody was the type of person she was, or things could've been worse.

One thing about her, she was gone always hold herself down, no matter how she had to do it. The girl was tough and wasn't to be fucked with, so I wasn't surprised when she told me how she got herself out of the situation. T-Bank was a trifling ass bitch, and Raheem and Bishop should've killed him when they had the damn chance.

"He's still recovering from surgery, but they said he's making progress. He's just been sleeping a lot because of the medicine they put in his IV. I feel like shit, Munchie. I really do. I could've got him and his daughter killed. I don't think I can ever forgive myself for that. He's such a good dude, and he deserves better than this, better than me. You know?" She looked over at me with teary eyes.

"I understand how you're feeling, but you can't beat yourself up over somebody else's actions. That's not fair to you. We talked about this before. Don't let T-Bank win. You're still in control of your own life. Y'all made it out alive, and that bastard will be going to jail for attempted murder," I snapped.

"I know, but just knowing he's in this same hospital as well got me on edge."

"He can't hurt you, Jody. Didn't you say the police was outside his door?"

"Yeah, but I wish the bullet had went through his fuckin' skull instead of in his damn shoulder. Why da fuck would he come back and do this shit to me? I know I kept Sunny a secret, but I thought I was doing what was best for us. Now I don't know if that was the right call or not. And on top of all this shit, Rissa is laid up in a damn coma," she said, getting choked up.

"Wait, what?" I asked.

"Bishop didn't tell you she was found in her home shot in the chest and had to be rushed to the hospital?"

I bit the inside of my jaw because Bishop hadn't told me shit like that. Everybody was laid up at the same damn hospital, and I was ready to go. But it was only one reason he would keep something like that away from me. He had to be the one to shoot her ass, and I wanted to know what happened between the two of them for him to try to kill her. It was so many secrets between the two of us we were starting to drown in each other lies.

"No. He didn't mention it. Where's Bella?" I questioned.

"She's mostly been with Rissa's mama, but Bishop has been getting her at night. How you didn't know any of this?"

"Because Bishop doesn't tell me shit. But that would explain why he hasn't stayed the last couple of nights. I'm sorry to hear that happened to her though."

"No the fuck you not. You don't have to fake it for me, but that's still my family. It's just too much shit going on at once. All I want is peace and to get the fuck away from here. I can't take this shit no more. I swear I can't. I worked hard to get myself on track, and now it's like I've been knocked right off that motherfucker."

"I know how you feel," I sighed.

Raheem hadn't been back to the hospital since Brandy caught us kissing. I tried to text her to see if she could call me, but she told me to delete her damn number. I guess I couldn't blame her at all. I didn't know what Raheem said to her to get her not to tell Bishop, but I was thankful. That was one less thing I had to worry about, but I'd made this bed, and I was trying my best not to lay in it.

I knew I was wrong, and so did Raheem, but it wasn't shit we could do about that now but figure out a solution. And maybe I was to blame for everything, but Bishop damn sure played his part in it too. When it came to revenge, it was mine to get back any fucking way I wanted to. That bastard deserved it because I was a down ass bitch for him, and he hurt me bad, but I guess that was why my ass was in the current situation I was in. Shit wasn't so sweet anymore, and I had a child to worry about. Therefore, I would figure it out one way or another.

"Well, let me get back to Stunna's room. His mother just flew in today, and she's supposed to be on her way here now. I'm nervous as shit," Baby Jo said, standing up.

"Why you nervous?" I questioned.

"Because I never met her before, and we was supposed to do Thanksgiving dinner, but now the first time I will meet her is in a fucking hospital because I got her son shot. Do you know how fucked up that is? I should just run while I still got the chance."

"It's not your fault, and if she doesn't understand, then fuck her!"

"Munchie, it's not always fuck everybody. When you go around telling yourself that, you tend not to think about how shit will play out, which is how you ended up in the situation you in with Raheem."

"Don't start." I rolled my eyes.

"You know I got your back, but you better slow da fuck down

and start thinking about your moves before you make 'em. That shit with Brandy could've ended worse. Keep ya chin up, boo, and yo' head on tightly. Lord knows you gonna need it."

"Girl, I swear we can give each other advice but can't help our-damn-selves." I laughed and got up to hug her after I laid BJ in the bassinet.

"We gon' be alright... I hope."

"We will," I assured her, even though I only halfway believed it for myself.

"Love you," she said right as the doctor walked in.

"Love you too. Call me later if you can."

"I will," she agreed before she left.

I talked with the doctor for about fifteen minutes, and then he gave me my discharge papers and had a nurse come in with a wheelchair for me and BJ. Luckily, by the time we made it outside, Bishop was pulling up. He got out the car and helped us get inside, and once everyone was situated, he pulled away from the hospital.

"You good, baby?" he questioned and glanced over at me.

"Why the fuck you ain't tell me 'bout Rissa?"

"Munch, we can discuss that shit later. I gotta go pick my daughter up, and I don't want that shit on my mind."

"I know you fucking shot her, but you fucked up because if she wakes up from that coma, she's going to take us all down, and you can believe that shit," I said, and that gave his dumb ass something to think about. Rissa knew too much, and I would bet my last dollar if she woke up, she would have a vendetta. Love was a twisted game, but I never thought it would get so wicked.

❧ 5 ❧

BABY JO

I sat in the chair beside Stunna's bed, looking at him as he slept. I tried to believe Munchie when she said everything was going to be okay for us, but wasn't nobody coming to save our asses. We'd been saved one too many times, and eventually, our luck was going to run out. It didn't matter how hard women like us tried, because the bullshit would always find its way back to us. We were better off giving the fuck up, but me, Stunna, and our girls were all still alive, so that was enough to make me keep a little bit of faith. Still, I was tired.

I was fed up with my life, and I was fed up with shit always going wrong for me. I felt like God was playing a sick game on me, and tears rolled down my cheeks as I silently prayed for mercy. I hadn't talked to God since I was a teenager and had all the faith in the world. Unfortunately, life snatched that shit right the fuck out of me and made me question everything, but I needed Him, and I needed him bad. The way I felt wasn't something I would be able to shake on my own. I was defeated, and it was crazy how one encounter with T-Bank could drag me right back to that dark place I'd fought so hard to get out of.

I was lucky it was just a neighbor knocking on my door the other day. When I walked outside, I discovered T-Bank had crashed into a cop's car trying to flee the scene. It was odd to witness, and I was in distress about a lot of things. A lump formed in my throat, and I just broke down right there. I buried my face in my hands and begged myself to get it the fuck together. But when the one thing I thought I escaped came back to haunt me, it took a toll on me and my mental. It didn't matter how many times I heard the shit wasn't my fault. It didn't change the way I felt.

Unlike a lot of motherfuckers, I could take accountability for my fuckups, and it was a lot of shit I could've done to prevent Stunna from getting shot. He tried to protect me, and I let my fear of T-Bank cloud my judgment and make me make dumbass decisions. I would've felt better if I was the one to take those bullets because Stunna simply didn't deserve it. I did. I waited until it was too late to leave T-Bank. I waited until we had a child, knowing that would tie me to that man for life. I couldn't change the past, but I damn sure did regret it.

"Oh, my baby," I heard an older woman say at the door, and I quickly wiped my face and sat up in my chair. When I did, I saw a gorgeous woman who resembled Viola Davis. I sniffed and stood up to greet her. "You must be Jody. I've heard a lot about you," she said and walked right over to me.

She threw her arms around my neck, and I stood there stiff as a board as she hugged me tightly. That was the last thing I was expecting from her. If anything, I expected her to walk in and slap the hell out of me and tell me everything was all my fault. I knew that was what I would've done if I were in her position. When she finally pulled away, she reached in her purse and pulled out a Kleenex before passing it to me. I took it from her and wiped the tears that just wouldn't stop.

"I am so sorry."

"Sweetie, you don't have a thing to be sorry about. Thank you for texting me and filling me in on what was going on. My baby is going to be alright, and you are too. I serve a mighty God, and I knew once I put it in His hands I didn't have a thing to worry about. When you have faith, there's no room for worry. I can see all in your face that you blame yourself, but God makes no mistakes, and my son won't hold this against you. He loves you. I can tell by the way his face lights up when he talks about you," she said and grabbed my shoulder in a motherly way as she looked me in my eyes. "God's grace is all you need to get through this. Don't allow the devil to take your joy. He comes to kill, steal, and destroy. Tell him he can't have you, because you're a child of God. Things may look bad now, but baby, he has a purpose for your life. Why do you think you've been under attack for so long?" she asked, and I wondered how she even knew that. "Your biggest battles comes before you biggest blessings." She winked, making me want to cry all over again because before she arrived, I was ready to relapse and go find myself some cocaine to take the pain away. But for some reason, when she told me everything would be alright, I believed her.

"Thank you so much. You just don't know how bad I needed to hear those words," I said, and it was like God answered my prayers right away and showed me that He was there for me after all. I was no saint, and I wouldn't pretend to be one, but He knew where my heart was.

"He might not come when you want Him—"

"But He'll be there right on time," I said, finishing her sentence, and her eyes lit up.

"You're going to be the perfect daughter-in-law." She smiled and rubbed my arm before she dropped her hand.

"I doubt I'll ever get a ring after all this." I laughed. "But Ajay is with my mother and my daughter, Sunny. I can go pick her up for you if you'd like."

"Okay. That sounds good, and maybe we can all go and grab a bite to eat later on, but I'm going to sit with my baby for a while," she said and looked over at Stunna. I nodded.

"I'd like that. I'm going to give you two time, and I'll be back in a little bit with the girls."

"Alright, sweetie," she said, patting my arm before she took my seat next to Stunna's bed. I watched as she bowed her head and laid her hands on him. I smiled and walked out the room to head to the elevators.

Once I made it to the waiting room, I walked through it and out the entrance doors. As soon as I did, I immediately wanted to turn around. I tried to hold my head down as I walked on the sidewalk and waited for the traffic to clear so I could make it across the street to my car. Unfortunately, holding my head down didn't do too much to disguise me. I took a deep breath because the fucking devil was busy today.

"Bitch! I know you hear me." Someone pulled on my arm hard.

"Getcho fuckin' hands off me, lady!" I yelled.

"You shot my son! Yo' ass is going to jail, you trifling ass bitch. You think you better than him now because you moved down here to Miami, huh? You ain't shit! Ain't never been shit and will never be shit," she said like I wasn't from Miami to begin with.

"Mrs. Brown, get the fuck out of my face," I said calmly. "And I'm not goin' to jail. It was self-defense. The only person getting locked up is yo' crazy ass son when he's discharged."

"If he's goin' down, you best believe I'm taking yo' ass down too. You kept my granddaughter away from us for all this time, and that shit is illegal. But we'll see if you still have that little smirk on your face when we file for custody and take her away from your crackhead ass. I have enough dirt to bury you, bitch! Do you hear me?" she asked, pointing at me.

The thought of them trying to take my daughter infuriated me. They'd done nothing but use and abuse me the whole time I was around them, and suddenly she wanted to come with threats? I stepped in her face and looked down my nose at her.

"I don't know what type of dirt you think you got on me, but I've been clean for years now. I turned my whole life around for that little girl, so it'll be a cold day in hell before you or him ever take her away from me. I don't owe you motherfuckers shit but my ass to kiss. Stay the fuck away from me and my child, or you gon' see some shit you ain't never seen before. I can promise you that," I said and then jogged across the street to my car before she could respond. She was lucky I'd just had that talk with Stunna's mama, or I would've stomped a hole in her ass. I'd put up a tough act in front of her, but as soon as I got inside my car, I broke down all over again, but that would be the last time, and I promised myself that.

6

MUNCHIE
A FEW MONTHS LATER

I peeked my head inside BJ's nursery, and once I saw he was still asleep, I tiptoed away from the door and went downstairs. I had on leggings with an oversized T-shirt, and a silk scarf was tied around my hair. It was safe to say I looked like shit, but I didn't even care. So much had gone on over the last few months, and I was truly exhausted. Between jumping up in the middle of the night to feed BJ and tending to Bella, I barely had time for myself. Things were rapidly changing, and I'd been putting everyone else's needs before my own.

Taking care of another woman's daughter was new to me. I didn't have a problem with Bella, and I would never treat her differently, but I was a first-time mother and had to figure shit out by the day. It wasn't easy, and I found myself crying more than anything else, but that was over with. I'd wiped my tears and vowed to make my next move my best move. Thanksgiving had come and gone, and so had Christmas, my birthday, and New Year.

I wish I could say those days had been wonderful, but honestly, I was glad to see the shit go. After that came my three-year anniversary with Bishop, but we didn't bother with much of a celebration. How could we when I was constantly busy with the kids? And truthfully, I was thankful for that. The last thing I wanted to do was celebrate some shit I was trying to figure my way out of. Bishop was pretty understanding and settled on cooking us dinner. Other than that, that was it.

Then Bella's first birthday popped up, and it was a huge reminder of when my life got turned upside down. After I discovered Rissa was pregnant, things changed for the better and the worse... but mostly for the damn worse. It hadn't been shit but a bunch of lying and sneaking around going on since that day. An entire year passed by that quickly, and it was funny how my first year home turned out nothing like I planned when I was locked up. That was why I took it one step at a time, and my next move was getting into my own place. I waited until after the holidays passed, but I couldn't wait any longer.

Rissa ended up never waking up from her coma, and she'd died last month. I wanted to be hateful and say fuck her, but the shit was sad as hell. I knew it was better if she didn't wake up, but I didn't expect to feel any type of way because she didn't. I was wrong, and it was kind of a hard pill to swallow. I figured it was because Bishop was the one who'd shot her and took her away from their child. He didn't even love her, and he'd done that, so I could only imagine how he would take the betrayal of someone he did love.

I could barely look him in the face most days, but he was barely home for me to do it anyway. He'd been so busy with Raheem out in the streets, and I couldn't say I missed the shit. He'd been asking when I would be ready to get back out there with him, but I had no plans of returning. Ever. I wasn't about to keep putting my life in danger for him when I had a son to worry about. I didn't give a fuck what he said or threatened to do, but I was fed the fuck up and decided I would do shit my own way.

I didn't have time to worry about how Bishop would react. We weren't doing shit but getting older, and time was passing us by so fast I could hardly believe it. But I'd done a lot of thinking and self-evaluating over the last few months. Although I couldn't change everything overnight, I had to start somewhere, and that was right where the hell I was. I walked into the kitchen and pulled out some leftovers before popping them into the microwave and then going to take a seat at the island. I grabbed my phone that had been sitting on the counter and dialed Baby Jo's number. I waited for her to answer, and when she didn't, I ended the call. It wasn't even a minute later before she started calling back. I picked my phone up and answered it.

"Hello?"

"You called me?" she questioned.

"No."

"Yes you did." She laughed, and I smiled.

"Well, what you asked if I called for? You know I called. What you doing?"

"I'm on the way to the airport to pick Stunna up. What you doing?"

"Nothing. About to eat something, and then I need to jump in the shower before BJ gets up. But I was calling to see if you knew anyone who needed a job and is good with kids."

"I told you to let my mama to do it. She has Sunny now."

"Yeah, I know, but I don't want to put too much on her. Plus, I'm still going to need a permanent babysitter."

"Girl, I told you to go through that damn website I sent you. They have plenty of qualified nannies and shit. You just have to pick who you want and set up an interview, but I can call my mama and get her to watch BJ for you tonight if you'd like."

"Yeah, that would be helpful," I said as someone started to ring the doorbell.

"Okay, I'll text you and let you know. Let me get off here," she sighed.

"What's wrong?"

"Nothing. I'll hit you in a lil' bit," she said and then hung up.

I looked at the phone for a second and then placed it down before getting up and going to open the door. When I did, I came face-to9face with Raheem, and he smiled at me. I moved to the side so he could come in and then closed the door back. He threw his arms around me and gave me a hug, and before he could kiss me, I stepped back and threw my hand up in his face.

"Don't even do that shit here. What brings you by?" I questioned.

"Damn, what's wrong with you?" Raheem frowned. "And where is my son?"

"Nothing, but I don't want to put myself in a position to get caught doing a damn thing, and I've told you that. He's upstairs sleeping." I walked off and went to the kitchen, and he followed me. He took a seat at the island while I pulled my plate out the microwave and went to take a seat across from him after grabbing a fork.

"Oh, okay, and chill. Bishop told me to meet him here. Said he was dropping Bella of at Rissa's mama's house, and then he would be back. So I knew he wasn't here."

"I don't care. Don't do that," I said before shoving my fork in my mouth.

"You seem upset." He stared at me.

"I'm exhausted. That's all."

Raheem and I were in a full-blown relationship behind Bishop's back, and that was another reason I had to get out of his house. It was just that time, and my biggest mistake was continuing to stay after everything I knew and did. I was done feeling bad about my actions. I could continue to sulk and feel sorry for myself while regretting shit, or I could move the fuck on with my life and take it for what it was. I loved Raheem, and he always stood on anything he told me. He didn't just say shit to hear himself talking.

"I know, but everything about to get better real soon. Here," he said and slid a key across the counter. I quickly picked it up and shoved it in my bra. "You ready to move?" he questioned, and my eyes got big.

"Can you hush? I still haven't told Bishop," I hissed.

"Told me what?" Bishop questioned as he walked into the kitchen out the blue, and I cursed myself for not turning the alarm system back on so it would've announced when he came in.

❦ 7 ❦

BISHOP

I looked at Munchie and Raheem and waited for her to answer my damn question. She was always somewhere trying to whisper about some shit or just avoiding me completely. I knew she'd been in her feelings ever since I shot Rissa, but I didn't see why the fuck she cared so much. Rissa not waking up from that coma was a good thing, and she was the one who had been on my back about the situation from the jump. Then when the bitch finally died, Munchie wanted to get in her feelings and have some sympathy all of a sudden.

I didn't know if it was her hormones or what, but she had a real nasty attitude lately. I tried to give her a pass, and I was happy to get the hell away from her whenever I could. She thought she was the only one tired, but that wasn't the fucking truth. She wasn't doing shit but sitting on her ass in the house with kids all day. That was nothing compared to the work Raheem and I was having to put in out in the streets.

We weren't having to deal with any flaw ass niggas, but we were having trouble keeping our folks supplied. They were running out of work faster than we could supply it, and that shit fell on my plug. If he couldn't keep up with my orders, I couldn't keep up with my people's needs and demands. The streets were booming, and if my plug didn't get that shit together, I was going to have to find somebody who could keep up. I had the money, and I wasn't about to keep waiting just because my plug was dealing with some shit.

When things slowed up like that, it meant it was a problem somewhere, but that problem wasn't mine, and I was ready to jump ship. I had too much to do to worry about my work being short. My distributors were pissed and hitting my line daily about needing more work. I couldn't even deal with that shit today though, because we were finally having the grand opening for the casino tonight. It was so much paperwork that came with that shit. I was starting to get frustrated, and with everything I had going on, she wanted to complain about not having help with the kids.

I didn't know how the fuck her dumb ass expected me to help her. I'd told her over and over again to hire a fucking babysitter, house cleaner, and whatever else she needed, but she hadn't done shit. Not a thing but sit on her ass and complain about nothing. She had it easy, and I felt like she was trying to stall. I needed her ass back out in the streets with me. Fuck everything else.

That money wasn't going to make itself, and I reminded her of that daily. She knew what it was before she had my son, so I didn't know why she was trying to act like the ultimate home-maker, because she wasn't. It had been three damn months already, and that was more than enough time for her to bounce back. She was walking around looking any kind of way and not even taking care of her-damn-self. I loved her, but she needed to do damn better. Everything I did was for us, and what the fuck was she doing? Not a damn thing. That was what.

"So don't nobody hear me talking?" I snapped.

"I was just telling Raheem that I've decided to move out," she said, dropping her fork, and Raheem looked like he was scared I was going to snatch her ass up, and he was right. Who did she think she was playing with? Somewhere along the line,

Munchie got it in her head that she was in control, and that shit was sexy at first, but those days, it wasn't doing shit but getting on my fucking nerves. Everything about her since we left the hospital with BJ was irritating my fucking soul, but I couldn't quite put my finger on what it was.

"You wanna say that again?" I quizzed, walking around the counter where she was at.

"Bruh, chill out," Raheem said, standing up, but I ignored his ass.

"Say," I asked, grabbing her arm roughly. Today wasn't the fucking day for the bullshit. It was supposed to be a good day, but of course, she was going to find a way to ruin that shit for a nigga.

"I said I'm moving out. It's been time to do so. We both know this shit with us isn't doing anything but getting worse. I can't take it, so I'm leaving for my own sanity," she calmly explained like she had everything figured out.

"You can't take it? I'm da one who has to put up wit' yo' fuckin' nagging. You knew the plan before we had BJ, and now you just mope around here looking fuckin' pathetic every day. Look at you! You look a damn mess."

"Excuse me!" she yelled and snatched her arm away from me. "I don't have time to worry about my looks when I'm busy taking care of the kids every day. I was waiting to see if Baby Jo's mama could get BJ before I went and fixed myself up for tonight, but I ain't got to explain shit to you. What the fuck do you do for the kids? What kind of help you giving? But you got the nerve to walk yo' black ass in here and talk to me crazy about my appearance? Get the fuck out my face, Bishop!" she yelled, shoving me in the chest, and before I knew it, I had her ass pinned against the wall.

That was how shit had been going for us. We didn't even get along anymore. I thought a baby would make our situation better and bring us closer together. Instead, it was pushing us further away from each other and causing problems. A baby didn't fix shit, and I should've realized that after my situation with Rissa. But everything happened so fast, and before I knew it Munchie was pregnant, and now we were here in this fucked-up predicament. It wasn't even five o'clock yet, and I already needed a damn drink and a fat ass blunt.

"Why you wanna fuck wit' me today, huh?" I asked, spitting in her face as I talked. She pissed me the hell off just that quick. "I thought you was better than this shit. I thought you was stronger, but I guess I was wrong. You ain't shit but a weak ass, codependent ass bitch! You like to pretend that you got it all together, but I know you, and I see right through you. As soon as shit get rough, you want to run. Oh, then you ready for change. Then you want to get yo' life together and boss up. Well, let me tell yo' ass this... You ain't bossed up on shit without da help of me. And now you wanna move out after I've sat here and gave yo' ass all of me?" I questioned.

She knew what she was to me and what she meant to me, and it was like she didn't even care. She never really gave me the chance to fix the shit, because before I could fix anything between us, she was complaining about the next damn problem. I tried to do better by her, but what about me? A nigga was losing his fucking mind right in front of her, and it was like she didn't give a fuck about me no more. We'd killed people together and all kinds of shit, but for some reason, I could tell she thought she was above me.

And in some ways, she was, but she was forgetting one important thing. When I met her, she was just as fucked up as I was on the inside. She was killing niggas before she met me. I didn't put that monster in her, because it was already there. I knew more about Munchie than she knew about her-damn-self. I was the nigga that studied every detail about a motherfucker, so she couldn't bullshit me.

"Bruh, snap da fuck out of it," I heard Raheem say as he roughly pulled me away from Munchie. "You fuckin' trippin'!" he yelled. I looked at Munchie, expecting to see tears in her eyes or rolling down her cheeks, but instead, she glared at me, not blinking once. She looked like she wanted to kill me, and although I didn't take the look as a threat, it was still weird as hell because I knew exactly how she felt.

"Yo, why you always in our fucking business!" I barked at Raheem. "This my wife! You ain't got no muthafuckin' right to step in between shit. When it comes to her," I pointed at Munchie, "you mind yo' gah damn business! I can handle mine." I nodded my head.

"Nigga, you in here doing all that shit for what? If she wanna leave, let her!" he yelled in my face, and Munchie was quick to get in between us.

"Relax! Raheem, go outside and let me talk to my husband in private," she demanded.

"Y'all got it," Raheem said, then looked at both of us before walking off.

"Now what da fuck made you think it was okay to tell that nigga anything before you told me?" I questioned.

"When have I had the time, Bishop? You're always in and out of here. You don't talk to me, and you don't want to be bothered with me. So I think it's best if BJ and I leave. You can do what you want after that. I honestly don't give a fuck." She folded her arms across her chest.

"Bae, what's done got into you?" I asked, grabbing her, and she rolled her eyes. I knew I had lost my cool a few seconds ago, but damn, a nigga was frustrated with her bullshit. Then her telling Raheem shit before me didn't make it no better. What went on between us needed to stay between us, unless I decided to let the nigga know what was going on. He was my homeboy, not hers, and that was where she'd crossed the fucking line.

"You don't know what you want. You're fed up with me, and I'm fed up with you. We don't need to be around each other. This shit is unhealthy for the baby, and I'm done dealing with it. I'm not happy, so I'm not staying. It's not up for debate."

"You really wanna leave, Munch?" I questioned, tilting my head to the side to look at her.

"I *am* leaving. It's not if I want to. I already have a place."

"So you went behind my back with this shit? What about me and Bella?"

"What about me and BJ, Bishop!" she yelled.

"You know what, Munchie? You can do whatever da fuck you wanna do!" I yelled in her face and then walked out.

8

BABY JO
LATER THAT NIGHT

"Jody," Stunna said, glancing over at me.

"Yes," I questioned, watching the road as he drove.

After I picked him up from the airport earlier, we went back to my place, and I called my mama to see if she could watch BJ for Munchie. When she agreed, I hit Munchie up to let her know, and then I chilled with Stunna until it was time for us to get ready for the grand opening. We were finally on our way there, and I was excited for the guys. I'd witnessed how hard they'd been working to make the shit happen, especially the last couple of months because they didn't think it was going to be up and running on time, and it wasn't.

The casino was actually supposed to open at the beginning of the month, but things got pushed back a couple of weeks. They still managed to make it happen, and that was all that mattered. Stunna had a pretty quick recovery after being shot by T-Bank. He had been shot in the leg, and a bullet grazed the side of his stomach. Luckily, neither shot was life threatening, and the doctor told Stunna he must've had a guardian angel because the bullet didn't hit an artery or vein.

It was a pretty clean shot, and after a couple of months of physical therapy, he was back to his normal self. Although, he did walk with a slight limp now like he was a pimp. I thought it was funny, and I was just happy that it wasn't worse. Yet I was still dealing with my own guilt, and I could tell it was starting to take a toll on my relationship with Stunna. I wasn't trying to push him away purposely, but my actions said differently. I just didn't feel like I deserved him anymore.

"What's up wit' you, boo?" he asked, and I frowned as he made a turn at the light.

"What do you mean?"

"Don't do that shit."

"What?" I raised my eyebrows.

"Don't act like you don't know what I'm talking 'bout."

"But I don't," I countered.

"So you gon' make me break da shit down? Jody, you been acting different ever since we left that hospital a few months ago."

"How? I've been here for you the whole entire time!" I yelled like he was accusing me of cheating or something.

"Why are you yelling?" he asked calmly, making me feel a little crazy.

"Sorry, but I really do feel like I've been here for you," I reasoned.

"And you have. That's not what I'm saying," he said and kept his eyes on the road as I looked at the side of his face.

"So what are you saying, Stunna?"

"I feel like you trying to push me away or some shit. Yeah, you've been here, but you ain't been here, ya feel me? You snapping on a nigga and starting pointless ass arguments wit' a nigga 'bout nothing. I don't do da drama or none of the extra shit, cuz I'm not gon' bring no extra shit in yo' life."

"So you feel like I brought some drama in yo' life? Matter fact, don't even answer that. I know I did, and I regret it every day."

"Again, that's not what I'm saying. Everything I'm telling you right now is referring to what happened after we left the hospital, not before we got there. You keep beating yo'self up about this shit, and I don't understand why. It wasn't yo' fault, but I know you still felt guilty cuz my daughter was there. I gave you weeks to get yourself together and get over that guilt you're feeling, but that shit ain't work, even when I've told you, you ain't got shit to feel guilty 'bout. It ain't like you set me up, and you was only doin' what you could to protect me the day that nigga popped up. But that's where you fucked up at. You ain't 'posed to be tryin' to protect a nigga. It's my job to protect you, and instead of you following my lead, you did yo' own thing. You already know I ain't no gangster ass nigga, so no, I didn't have a gun on me. For one, my daughter was wit' me, and I didn't want that shit nowhere near her. So I was lacking, and that was my fault. I didn't know how fucked up that nigga really was in the head. Somebody like that never deserved you."

"And I don't deserve you!" I blurted out, unable to hold on to the feelings any longer since my actions were betraying me anyway.

"I ain't shit special, Jody. And if I felt any type of way about what happened, I would've walked away months ago. You da only one still holding on to that shit, and again, I understand you feel guilty for putting my daughter in danger, but you have to accept what's already happened. And yes, maybe if you had been anybody else, I would've walked away and never spoke to you again. But you worth everything you come with. Let a nigga unload that baggage though cuz it's not gon' stop shit this way. We both know we not gon' play 'bout our kids, and they come first, but after them, we have each other. We all survived, and you gon' have to learn how to listen and stop fuckin' fighting me on everything. I'm not that other nigga, and I ain't gon' ever do shit to hurt you purposely. I only say purposely cuz I feel like all relationships have their problems. That's just what come wit' da shit. Ain't nobody perfect. So check this out, you gon' stop playing wit' me and let somebody love yo' mean ass," he said, finally pulling up to the casino that was already packed as hell.

"Somebody?" I questioned.

"Me, nigga!" he yelled, and I fell out laughing.

"Mhm." I nodded my head, and he grabbed my hand after parking in the back.

"I already love you, Jody. You not gon' get rid of me that easily. Let that guilt go so we can move on," he said, reaching over and grabbing my chin. He looked me in my eyes, and I knew he was being genuine. He was right about everything, and I guess all I needed was for him to clarify that he didn't hold it against me. I mean, he'd already said that, but he'd finally laid out exactly how he felt about everything, and that made me feel better. I trusted him, and as I looked at him, it was like I felt the guilt leave my body right there and then.

"I love you too, Stunna," I finally said, and he leaned in to kiss my lips.

"Come stay wit' me in Vegas for a lil' bit when I leave here. You and Sunny both. A change of scenery is what you need, and I'm going to give it to you."

"Are you asking me or telling me?" I smirked at him.

"I'm tellin' you. You a strong ass woman, and you can hold yourself down, and that's what I admire about you. But you ain't got to be strong for me, baby. Let somebody else carry that load while you kick back and enjoy life with no worries. I got you, and I'ma keep assuring you of that until you get that shit through yo' big ass head. You hear me?" he asked, and I smiled.

"I can let you lead, but if you crash, I'm getting back in the driver's seat," I joked, but he didn't laugh.

"If I crash, I'ma get that shit towed, get a rental, and get back on the road until that car is repaired. Ya feel me?" He smiled, showing all his teeth.

"Come on, witcho crazy self." I laughed, opening the door, but I understood exactly what he was saying. If shit somehow got fucked up between us, he was willing to fix it, and that was all someone like me could ask for. I'd been giving him a tough time, hoping he would give up on me and find someone more deserving of him, but he didn't do that. And although we hadn't had sex, the nigga was touching my soul and didn't even know it. I'd been hesitant to give myself to him, but he was definitely getting some pussy at the end of the night.

Stunna hopped out of the car after telling me to wait for him, and then he walked around to my side and opened the door. I placed my hand in his and allowed him to help me out of the car. I had on a black fur jacket along with a Saint Laurent one-shoulder mini dress that was black and hugged the little curves I had. On my feet were a pair of black red bottoms, and I had a clutch purse that was shaped like red lipstick. Next to me, Stunna was dressed in a Dolce & Gabbana three-piece suit with a Cuban link chain around his neck, fat diamonds in his ears, and a Richard Millie on his wrist.

My man was looking real daddyish, and I felt like the hood Cinderella as we made our way in the back door after walking through security. There were cameras all over the place, and they could easily be spotted so a nigga knew not to try a damn thing. They hired actual security guards, but among them was hood niggas with the same shirts on, and they were waiting for a nigga to jump stupid. We could never be too sure, especially not with the shit that had been going on with us. T-Bank was behind bars where he belonged, and I was still waiting to see how much time he would get for attempted murder and attempted kidnapping.

Not only that, but the fool also had drugs in the car, and they were slapping him with any and everything. Stunna's expensive lawyer was making sure of that, and I knew when it was all said and done, T-Bank was going away for a long time. That bitch disgusted me, and I was happy to see that he and his mother were getting exactly what they deserved. I might've broke down in my car that day outside of the hospital, but a few days after that, I went and got a restraining order on her ass. Of course I had to act like I feared for my and Sunny's lives, and I told them she was the one who told T-Bank where to find me in the first place.

I expected them to give me a hard time, but money was the motive, and I got that restraining order quick as hell. Mrs. Brown didn't know that when she actually tried to go file for custody of Sunny on T-Bank's behalf. Them people laughed in her fucking face and basically told her that shit wasn't happening. The battle was over before it started, and what made it even better was T-Bank and his mother were both out of my life for good. That chapter was closed, and I didn't plan to ever look back.

When we finally made it to the office, Raheem, Bishop, and Munchie were all waiting for us and looking like they wanted to kill one another. I didn't know what was going on, but I knew the truth couldn't have been out if they were all still alive and in the same room. We made small talk for a few minutes, and then we headed outside where a crowd of people were anxiously waiting for the grand opening. Bishop gave a speech with Raheem next to him while Munchie stood off to the side, looking like she wanted to be anywhere but there. And I was sorry, but the whole thing was cringey as hell knowing what I knew.

Munchie had really fucked herself over, but I told her I had her back, and I did. I wasn't a fool, and I knew Bishop was the one who killed Rissa. Ever since then, I made sure to keep my distance from his ass as much as possible. He was the godfather of my daughter, but I didn't want to be around him. He was just as much to blame for all of this shit as Munchie, and truthfully, I didn't know who was dumber.

I told myself I wouldn't judge, but at the same damn time, I was judging the hell out of all three of them. Somebody was going to die, and I couldn't see shit ending any other way. Stunna was right when he said I needed a change of scenery because I had to get away from the crazy ass shit the three of them had going on. Anyway, after Bishop gave his speech, Raheem said a few words, and then Stunna stepped up and thanked a few people before passing Bishop a big ass pair of scissors.

The red band in front of the building was cut, and then Bishop and Raheem pulled the doors open and started greeting people as they filed inside. The rest of the night went by pretty smoothly, and it was a real celebration, but shit did get a little weird when the chick named Dula showed up. Apparently, Bishop had ran into her somewhere and invited her. Munchie was pissed when she showed up, but that was before she found out she hadn't been invited by Raheem.

It was crazy because she felt better that Bishop had invited Dula and welcomed her with no problem afterward. I'd learned she was planning to move into her own spot, so I guess she really didn't give a fuck about Bishop anymore, and vice versa if he was allowing it to happen. Munchie talked with her old friend for the majority of the night, and they caught up with one another's lives, but if I was Munchie, I wouldn't trust that bitch as far as I could throw her ass. Something wasn't right, but no one ever took heed to a warning until it was too late.

9

MUNCHIE
NINE MONTHS LATER

BJ's first birthday party was a few days away, and I couldn't believe my baby was about to turn one so soon. The time passed by quickly, and I was happy to have something to cheer me up. When I first moved out of Bishop's mansion, I expected him to beg me to stay, even after he told me to do what I wanted. Well, turned out, he meant that shit because I barely heard from him for a while.

He would hit me up occasionally to ask about BJ, but that was it. He didn't ask to stop by or see where I lived, and I'm not going to lie; that kind of stung. It was like he was completely over me and my shit, and it was something I wasn't used to. The Bishop I knew would've done everything in his power to stop me from moving out, but nope, not that time. Eventually, I didn't care at all, and I figured he'd found someone to entertain him in my absence. That was cool though because it made things a hell of a lot easier for Raheem and me.

He was the one who had been there, and things had been good. I wasn't stressed out, and I was able to enjoy my baby growing up in peace. I helped him learn to crawl, and he was walking at ten months. Now he was about to turn one, and I couldn't help but to tear up.

"Munchie, you good, babes?" Dula asked, and I nodded.

"Yes, I'm fine. I just can't believe he's about to be one," I said, smiling at BJ, who was playing with Dula's three-year-old nephew in the middle of my living room floor.

When Dula popped up at the casino's grand opening, I was livid, but I quickly discovered Bishop was the one who invited her. I didn't bother to ask where he ran into her at, because I really didn't care, but Dula eventually told me it was at the strip club. I wasn't surprised, because nothing Bishop did seemed to surprise me at that point. Anyway, I played nice with Dula because as far as Bishop knew, I didn't have a reason to be mad that she was there. As the night progressed, we just clicked all over again like we did when I first met her in prison, and we ended up having a good night.

After that, we started to hang out more, and her being Raheem's ex didn't bother me too much. Truthfully, they weren't talking for long, and I didn't have the right to be mad no way, so I squashed it, especially since Dula was the only person available whenever I wanted to talk or just have a day outside of the house. When Baby Jo first left to go to Vegas, I expected for her to be gone for a few weeks or so, but those three weeks had easily turned into nine months with her and Stunna only coming back to visit when it was necessary.

"They do grow up fast as hell. I remember my sister sending me pictures of my nephew when I was in prison, and now he's already three."

"It really is something," I agreed. I felt bad for Dula because she'd recently opened up to me about her not being able to have kids. It was something we'd never discussed while being locked up, but she said it was because having kids was the least of her worries during that time. Since she was out and free, it started to bother her, and I could tell. But before I could offer some encouraging words, BJ took the toy he was playing with and cracked it upside Dula's nephew's head. "BJ!" I yelled, hopping up to grab him. Ever since he started walking, he'd been getting into everything and doing anything. "See? You already messing up. But if I cancel yo' party, yo' lil butt gon' be crying," I fussed, and Dula laughed as she got up to grab her nephew, who was yelling.

"They're just being boys, Munchie. And we both know yo' ass ain't cancelling shit. Look at your backyard right now," she said, pointing through the patio doors.

I looked outside and started cracking up because she was right. I wasn't cancelling a thing, and I had BJ spoiled as hell. I wasn't nothing but talk when it came to my son, and I think he knew that because he stayed trying me. Yet there wasn't a thing he could do to get his first birthday party cancelled. I was having it in my backyard, and it was currently a team of guys making the whole yard look like something out of a superhero movie. We were planning to have people in costumes flying in the air and all on the day of the party, and I couldn't wait to see how everything turned out.

"You right. Plus, I can't wait for everyone to get together. It's been a while since... you know..." I said, my voice trailing off.

"I know what you mean. How's he doing?" Dula asked, bouncing her nephew in her arms as he glared at BJ, who was grinning like he'd done nothing wrong.

"Dula, I honestly don't know. Bishop was barely talking to me before, and then that happened, and he really shut me out. I was actually surprised when he texted asking about the plans for BJ's birthday party. He hadn't been concerned about BJ at all, but I wouldn't dare tell him he couldn't come to the party after what happened."

"Yeah, I don't think that would be the best idea either. Just let him come and play shit cool."

"Girl, that's the plan." I bit the inside of my jaw.

"Have you talked to Raheem?" she questioned, and I bit on my jaw harder.

The thing about becoming friends with Dula again was I had to hide my emotions about certain things. She didn't know anything about my situation with Raheem, and because she'd formed some type of feelings for him when they were together, I couldn't tell her. She just thought Raheem and I were really close because he was Bishop's best friend. So at times, she would ask about him or who he was talking to, and I would have to play shit out like I didn't know or care. I was okay with her being his ex, but I wasn't okay with being asked about him.

"No," I lied because I talked to him daily.

"Oh okay. You know I have to ask." She laughed a little, and I gave her a fake smile.

"As usual. I told you to forget him. Rah is going to be Rah, and he ain't even worth being thought about," I said as I finally placed BJ back down on his feet.

"You're probably right, but he's so damn fine, and I can't get that monster inside his pants off my mind. Every time I see him, I just wanna suck on it," she said and made some crazy ass sexual noise that made my skin crawl.

"What time you had to meet your sister?" I asked, looking at the clock on my wall, and Dula pulled her phone out.

"Oh shit. I got to go. Plus, I have a dick appointment I can't miss later while I'm sitting here thinking about Raheem's ass." She laughed.

"You're a mess." I waved her off and watched as she gathered their things.

After I walked her out I returned to the living room and plopped down on the couch. Although things had been good for me, that changed a few months ago when Bishop called me on the phone hollering. I could still hear the sound of his choked-up voice on that phone call. It was heart shattering, and no matter what we went through and did to each other, that was some shit I would've never wished on him. He didn't deserve no mess like that, but karma was a coldhearted bitch, and she didn't spare him at all.

I watched BJ playing and thought about how Bishop must've felt a few months ago when tragedy struck. He was at home with

Bella, and she was playing with her toys while he walked around on the phone handling business. He said he'd just hung up the phone call when he turned around and saw her choking on something. He tried to save her, but everything happened so fast, and before he knew it, she died right in front of him from choking on a plastic toy that got caught in her throat. The whole thing was terribly sad, and the funeral wasn't any better.

Our whole group came together to be there for him, but as soon as the weekend was over, he was quick to shut everyone out except for Raheem. That was why I was shocked he hit me up about BJ's birthday party because I hadn't heard from him since the death of his daughter. So the party was going to be the first time I saw him in a while, and I was nervous.

10

BABY JO
A COUPLE DAYS LATER

"You're always so good to me," I said, grinning at Stunna who was sitting across from me.

We'd landed in Florida last night with the girls and checked into a penthouse suite since I was renting out my condo. It was something I'd come up with to have my own income since Stunna basically kidnapped me after I went to Vegas with him. However, he didn't have to try hard because as soon as I got there, I felt like I was at home, and he made sure of that. It was so nice to be away from the drama.

I spent time with Sunny and Ajay daily while Stunna managed business. Ajay was no longer giving me a challenging time ,and she actually wanted to be around me. Stunna was right when he said she just needed time because the more I was around her, the more she welcomed me into her life. And now she and Sunny were calling each other *sister*, and Stunna and I thought that was the sweetest thing. Nothing compared to being happy and able to witness your child truly happy as well.

It was a new feeling, and it was like we'd become a blended family overnight. People often thought Stunna and I had been together forever and that Sunny and Ajay were both of our girls. In a way, they were, but we never bothered to explain anything to anyone. What was the point? We knew our situation, and that was the only thing that mattered.

Anyway, we were back in town for BJ's first birthday party, and the girls had gone to my mama's house for the night. Stunna didn't mind Ajay going over there, and when we were in Vegas, I allowed Sunny to go spend the night over his mother's house with Ajay. The two of them barely wanted to do anything without the other, so we didn't bother attempting to split them up. It was hard to believe almost a year ago Stunna got shot in my apartment by T-Bank. That was something I often tried to forget, but the situation made our relationship so much stronger, and I'd learned that if a man really wanted you, he would do anything to be with you.

Not only that, but Stunna was the most-forgiving and under-standing man I knew, and over time, he made me believe I actually deserved him. That was no longer a doubt in my mind, and matter fact, I didn't have many of those these days. That man had me sure of myself, and I loved that and him.

"I'ma keep being good to you." He smirked, and I knew what was on his nasty ass mind.

He'd arranged dinner on the rooftop of the hotel we were staying at, and the sun was currently setting. It was shit like that, that had me spoiled as hell by him because he never failed to amaze me when it came to a date night. And please believe he always made time to have at least a couple every single month. I couldn't even picture myself looking at another man, because everything I needed and wanted was right in front of me. Stunna was perfect in my eyes, even though he said it was no such thing, but had he seen himself?

"You betta," I joked and pushed my empty plate away.

"You want something else to eat?" Stunna questioned, and I shook my head.

"Boy, I'm stuffed."

"I got something to stuff yo' muthafuckin' ass wit'."

"Oh yeah?" I flirted with my eyes, and he smiled at me.

"Girl, don't make me come across this damn table on yo' sexy ass."

"You so stupid." I laughed because I knew he would really do that shit.

"Come sit on my lap," he said, pushing himself away from the table and holding his hand out for me.

I got up from my chair and walked over to him before sitting in his lap. He wrapped his arms around my waist and rested his chin on my shoulder. At times, I was convinced he didn't just call me baby and actually thought I was his damn baby. He always wanted to have me wrapped up in his arms, and most nights his ass rocked me to sleep. That shit brought me comfort, and I would be lying if I said I didn't love it.

It was something about it that made me feel wanted constantly or like he needed me just as much as I needed him. With him around, I didn't have to worry about the negative shit. And that was why I was never in a rush to get back to Florida. I missed my people like hell, but that toxic shit they had going on was draining, and I was glad to be away from it. Of course I was always just a phone call away, but sometimes, I just had to get the fuck away from people when they had too much going on.

That bullshit could overlap into my life, and I wouldn't have known what the hell was going on. But my mama had always taught me that being acquainted to the wrong things could also block your blessings, so it was certain thing I just had to be aware of. And there was nothing wrong with loving someone and being there for them from a distance. I would never turn my back on Munchie, but I knew she understood more than anyone how badly I needed the peace I'd finally found, and she'd managed to find some peace of her own. Well, that was until the situation with Bishop happened, and that shit still broke my heart.

Hell, I cried for him because it was fucked up. That was a lot coming from me because Bishop had been on my shit list for a while. He killed my cousin, and then my baby cousin died while in his care, but from a parent's perspective, I was able to sympathize. But if I was Bishop, Munchie, or Raheem, I'd be scared to do anything wrong because clearly they reaped what they sowed. We all were human, but in the end, I felt like it came down to a person's intentions.

"What you thinking 'bout?" I turned my head a little to look at Stunna because he was too quiet.

"I'm thinking 'bout you, baby. I know you think I just wanted to have a nice dinner date before the party tomorrow, but I actually wanted to talk to you 'bout some things."

"What's wrong?" I asked, alarmed.

"Ain't nothing wrong. How can it be when I got yo' fine ass right here?" He gripped my thigh.

"I don't know." I smiled goofily.

Although I was secure in my relationship, there was still a small part of me that was afraid of losing him. I feared he would wake up one day and decide he didn't want to be with me anymore. It didn't matter if I knew that was ridiculous, because that feeling crept up on me occasionally. Some shit like that would break my heart, and I didn't know if I would ever be able to trust again, but luckily, I had more faith than that.

"Jody, I love what we've built together in such a small amount of time. I know you've been through a lot, and I hope I've been able to play a part in making shit better for you. You know I'ma expressive nigga, and someone like you amazes me. I ain't just saying that shit either. You got a heart of gold, and I love the way you're always focused on your daughter and doing what's best for both of you. You're far from selfish, and that shit gon' take you far. And not only do you go beyond for your daughter, but you do the same with mine. I see the way you are with her, and she loves you. You treat her just like she's your daughter too, and you've brought a different type of happiness to her life. We were fine alone, but you gave her someone to look up to. You're showing her how a woman should carry herself, and..." he said and then paused for a second before continuing. "And you're giving her something she felt like she was missing. She has the best of everything, but what she didn't have was a mother. You came in and gave her that with no problem, and I can tell she's happier. It was days when she would ask about her mother, and I didn't know how to explain to a child that her mother didn't want to be a mother. Fuck man," he said, pausing again. "This shit wasn't supposed to be emotional." He laughed a little, and I shifted in his lap so I could reach around to rub his back. I understood exactly what he was saying because everything he said I'd been for his daughter, he'd been for mine. "I guess what I'm tryin' to say is I want you forever, and I want you to know it." He tapped my leg.

I stood up to see what was wrong, but when he dropped down to one knee, my eyes got big as hell, and my heart felt like it sank because I just knew like hell this man wasn't about to...

"Jody, will you marry me?" he proposed, pulling a ring out that had a fat ass diamond in the middle.

My hands flew up to my mouth, and tears started to roll down my face as I shook my head. He was fucking proposing, and although I was witnessing it, I still couldn't believe it. Was he serious? Did he really want to marry me out of all people? The cat had my damn tongue, and I couldn't say shit. I was sure I was standing there looking like a damn fool because what had I done to deserve this?

"Gahh damn, my knee starting to hurt niii. If you gon' hurt a nigga feelings, do it quick so I can get the hell up and jump off this balcony," he said, and I busted out laughing because he could never be serious.

"Yeah, fool. I'll marry yo' ass or whatever." I smirked, and he slid the ring on my finger before standing up to kiss me.

11

BISHOP
THE NEXT DAY

"Here, bruh," Raheem said, passing me the fat ass blunt we was smoking on.

We were sitting in his car outside Munchie's house. It was weird even saying that shit, and it was also my first time seeing her place. I was pissed the fuck off when she actually got her shit and moved out, but I didn't try to stop her. I saw the look in her eyes that day when she told me she was moving, and I knew if I didn't let her go, I was gon' end up killing her ass. It was certain shit I couldn't handle, so I did what was best for me and allowed her to leave.

If she thought that shit was gon' make her feel better, then that was on her. As soon as she moved out, I gave her the space she so badly wanted and didn't hit her up much. I just knew she would be running back to me in less than a month. What I didn't know was she was living in a nice ass house. I mean, it wasn't shit like my mansion, but it was way nicer than I expected.

"How in da fuck she can afford this?" I asked, looking over at Raheem.

"Right. This shit nice as hell," he said, looking out the

window at her crib. It was his first time seeing the shit too. "But you good though?" he questioned, and I hit the blunt harder.

"Nah, I'm not. I just want to get this shit over with," I admitted.

It was BJ's first birthday party, and although I should've been excited, I wasn't. It was hard for me to come and celebrate the birth of one child when I'd just lost one. That shit hurt me so fucking bad I didn't know how I was still making it. I was pissed the fuck off and full of remorse at the same damn time. The shit was taking me over and making it hard for me to focus.

I was more anxious out in the streets, and I'd started killing niggas for the smallest things. If a nigga looked at me wrong, he was dead. If a nigga questioned me, he was dead. There wasn't any major problem out in the streets, but I was making one every single day because killing motherfuckers made me feel a little better. It gave me a high and eased my nerves so I would be able to sleep at night.

Raheem had been trying to talk some sense into me, but there wasn't no point in doing that. That shit was dead. My daughter died right in front of me, even after I tried my fucking hardest to save her. It wasn't enough, and I was too late. The shit didn't seem fair at all. And I kept thinking about what I could have done differently. I was fighting with myself about killing Rissa because if she had still been alive, I was sure my daughter would be too.

Then I was pissed the fuck off because Munchie left me, and I felt like if she hadn't left, I would've had the help I needed. She left me on my own, me and my daughter both, and as a result my child was gone. Meanwhile, she was living in a mini mansion with our son stress free. That bitch thought I was just gon' allow her to be there for me when I didn't even want the hoe around me. Clearly, she had a nigga helping her out because I knew her pockets weren't that damn long.

Hell, I was still sending her money for our son even after she said fuck me. I might've not been there, but that was for my own good. Munchie let me down, and that shit had my heart heavy. Then again, it felt better to blame anyone but my-damn-self. I couldn't handle that.

"Bishop," I suddenly heard Rah calling my name, and I snapped out of my thoughts.

"Nigga, what?" I asked, annoyed.

"Don't you think we need to be heading in? The party started thirty minutes ago."

"Fuck that. Roll up again," I said, flicking the last bit of the blunt out the window. I'd smoked the rest of that shit up without bothering to pass it back to Rah. Hell, I needed it more than he did.

"Bruh, let's just go inside, and then we can smoke again later."

"I don't wanna fucking go in there." I was starting to regret hitting Munchie up to see what she had planned for him. I thought I could do this, but I was starting to feel sick to my damn stomach.

"Ay, dawg, I know this shit tough for you, but it's gon' be cool. Come on," he said, opening his door and getting out.

I was tired of his ass too, but he was the only motherfucker I could vent to. He knew what I'd been through and the shit I'd done. Unlike Munchie's ass, he didn't switch up on me. It was still some shit off about him though. I just couldn't figure out what the fuck it was, but what I did know was the nigga was different. He moved and acted different at times.

It was like he had some shit going on that he didn't want me to know about, but I assumed it had something to do with a hoe. Yet that wasn't the problem. The problem was him trying to hide the shit from me like we didn't pass these bitches back and forth at a point in time. And another thing that pissed me off was that he always tried to take up for Munchie and make me see shit from her point of view. I knew they'd gotten cool over time, but they weren't that damn cool.

"Fuck it," I said, opening my door too. I was just happy the nigga was with me because there was no way in hell I would've been able to go through attending the party by myself.

"My boy," Raheem said, patting my back sternly as I walked up beside him in front of the car. We walked up on the front porch, and Raheem rang the doorbell.

"Fuck that," I said, twisting the knob and letting us in. The shit wasn't locked no way, and I didn't give a fuck if it was. What the fuck I looked like knocking?

"Oh, hey, y'all," Munchie said, making her way to the door as we walked in. I saw her eyes go to our hands, and that was when I remembered I forgot to buy a damn gift.

"What's up, Munchie?" Raheem asked as she gave him a half hug and looked at me.

"Nothing much. Everyone is in the backyard."

"Cool," Raheem said, and then we both started to walk off, but Munchie grabbed my forearm.

"Can I talk to you for a minute?" she asked, and Raheem stopped walking to look at me.

"I'll meet you outside, bruh," I said, and then he looked at us both briefly before walking away and finding his way to the backyard.

"How have you been?" Munchie asked, looking concerned.

"What da fuck do you care?" I questioned.

"Bishop, I'm not tryin' to argue wit' you. I just wanted to check in and see how you was doin'. That's all."

"Oh, now you wanna check in? You ain't pulled up to da fuckin' house not once since the funeral!" I yelled.

"You wasn't answering my calls," she gasped, and I sucked my damn teeth at her stupid ass.

"I lost my fucking child! What da fuck does it matter! You knew where da fuck I was at, and all you did was try to reach me over da phone. If you was really concerned, you would've pulled yo' duck ass up, hoe. But we both know you on another nigga's dick now. Nice place, by the way," I said sarcastically.

"You know what? You got it. Like I said, I'm not tryin' to

argue wit' you. I gave you space just like you gave me. I know you're hurt, and I apologize for not being there."

"Bitch, fuck you! It's yo' fault my daughter dead. Get da fuck out my way so I can go see my son," I said and then shoved her ass to the side before I knocked her the hell out. She could stay the fuck out my face for the rest of the evening with her trifling ass. I was grieving my daughter while that hoe was getting fucked and not worried about my me or my feelings. Therefore, it was no need for her to try to fake give a damn now. *Bitch!*

"Bishop! What's up, dawg? How you feelin'?" Stunna asked as soon as I walked in the backyard, and I went over to slap hands with him.

"What's good, man? I'm surviving."

"That's all we can do, brother." He patted my shoulder.

"Hey, sis. You good?" I asked, hugging Baby Jo, and she rubbed my back.

"Yeah, but fuck me. I'm glad you doin' alright," she said as we pulled away.

I knew Baby Jo felt some type of way about me and the things I'd put Munchie through, but she didn't let that stop her from reaching out. Even when I didn't respond, she would still send texts saying she was just checking on me, and I appreciated that shit. Our brother-sister bond broke a long time ago, and we both knew it, but I'd always look out for her if she needed me. And to be honest, I thought Baby Jo had outgrown a lot of shit, and I couldn't do nothing but respect it. She was doing good for herself, and I was happy for her after everything she'd been through with T-Bank over the years.

I despised that nigga, but we weren't all that different, and a nigga sure as hell wasn't trying to crash out like he'd done. I knew I had to do better, but that shit seemed damn near impossible, especially with everything I was dealing with. I didn't need no sympathy either; I needed my fucking daughter back. That wasn't happening, so maybe I was just fucked.

"Rahh Rahh!" I heard a small voice yell, and then I saw BJ

run straight up to Raheem and put his arms up like he didn't see his fucking daddy. I didn't even know the little nigga was walking now, but I guess that was my own damn fault.

"What's up, lil' homie?" Raheem asked, scooping him up, and I frowned.

"Damn, you don't see yo' daddy, nigga?" I questioned, and that little fucker snatched his head away like he didn't know who the fuck I was. Yet he was running up, screaming Raheem's name and shit, and that didn't sit right with me, because Raheem's ass didn't see BJ no more than I did. "Come here, boy," I said, taking him from Raheem, and he got to yelling and trying to hit me in my face. He never did like me. "Ay! Cut that shit shit out before I whoop yo' ass out here. I don't know what yo' mama allow, but you don't hit nobody in they fucking face unless you wanna get hit back," I fussed as he wiggled all around. "And how da fuck my son know yo' name?" I asked Raheem. I had to get that shit off my chest without delay before I started assuming the worse.

"Man, that nigga said *roar roar* like he a monster or some shit. He don't know my damn name." Raheem laughed at me and shook his head and I felt crazy as hell.

"Oh, nigga I was 'bout to catch a muthafuckin' charge out here," I said, and everyone laughed, but I wasn't joking. "Happy birthday, man. Go play witcho crybaby ass," I said, putting him back down, and he took off running as Munchie walked in the backyard. He looked and acted just like her ass. That wasn't good.

"How is business?" Stunna asked as Baby Jo walked away to go talk to Munchie.

The backyard was big as fuck, and she had that shit set up straight. It looked like a city with chaos going on, and instead of buildings, there was bouncy houses everywhere. Niggas in super-hero costumes were flying around over the fake city, You couldn't pay me enough to dress up in no damn tights and do that shit. They were connected to straps, and behind the bouncy houses, it was people making sure shit didn't go wrong making their asses fall out the damn sky.

"It's goin' good, man. They love that shit around here, and once I added strippers, it really took the fuck off. Club Casino is da hottest thing around right now," I said to Stunna, and he nodded.

"That's what the fuck I'm talking about. I knew y'all was the niggas to come to with this shit. And Bishop, don't be afraid to take some time off if you need. Rah told me you be at that casino every day when y'all not on the road. You gots to have some time for yourself," he said, hitting my chest with the back of his hand.

"Man, all I got is time to my-fuckin'-self. Ain't nobody at da crib, so that's why I go to da casino," I said and then thought about the things that had been running through my head while I was alone. It was an everyday battle, and I didn't feel like I would ever be alright.

"I feel you." Stunna nodded his head and looked toward a bouncy house that Sunny, his daughter, and BJ were all jumping in along with a few other kids. I didn't even know why Munchie went all out. It wasn't like we was cool with a lot of people to begin with. I had many acquaintances, but friends? No.

"Da fuck she doin' here?" Raheem asked, watching as Dula walked in the backyard with a little boy. He got pissed off any time he saw her, but I didn't see what the hell he was mad about. He was the one who broke up with her ass.

"Shit, last I heard, she and Munchie was tight now."

"Nigga, I don't know why da fuck you invited that girl to the grand opening to begin with."

"Muthafucka, you told me y'all was still together."

"If that shit was true, I would've invited her my-damn-self."

"Well, I ain't know," I said, waving him off. Of course I knew because she told me, but he wasn't about to know that. "What da hell you lie 'bout that shit for anyway?" I interrogated.

"Cuz that's my fuckin' business."

"Oh, now you wanna talk 'bout what's yo' business? But anytime anything go on wit' me and my wife, you da first person to stick yo' nose in da shit. Even Baby Jo be minding her business, and she a female."

"I'm goin' to get me a damn drink."

"Yeah, a'ight," I said as he walked away. I had to keep my eyes on that nigga.

"Da fuck goin' on wit' y'all?" Stunna questioned, and I shook my head.

"It ain't shit. You know how me and Rah be."

"Well, y'all better keep that shit together. It seem like it's a lil' more goin' on. Y'all business partners now, and it's plenty of money to be made. Don't let me down nii. I got a lot of money invested in you niggas, and if y'all got to beefing on some crazy shit, that won't be good for business. You feel me?" he asked.

"Nigga, it ain't shit goin' on. We straight. Business is business. Shutcho ass up!"

"Good, 'cause we got a muthafuckin' wedding on da way, dawwwwg."

"Nigga, you lying!"

"I ain't lying 'bout shit. I rides for mine," he said, looking across the yard at Baby Jo. "You see that woman over there." He pointed.

"Yeah."

"Someone like her only comes once in a lifetime, and I ain't never be no fool. Stamped! Da fuck? Meet me at da alter in yo' white dress. We ain't getting' no younger. We might as well do it," he started singing in a fake microphone, and I started laughing at his clown ass.

"This nigga really popped da question. Congratulations. Now let's go celebrate," I said, throwing my arm over his shoulder, and we went to find some liquor. I sure as fuck needed it if I was going to stay.

Luckily, the rest of the party went by fast, and before I knew it, the sun had gone down. We'd sung happy birthday and fucked up the seafood bar. BJ opened gifts and helped cut his birthday cake. Munchie had smashed a piece in his face, and when I say that nigga started hollering loud as fuck like a little bitch, I meant it. Munchie was making him soft as hell, and she wasn't doing any kind of disciplining.

The more I watched him was the more irritated I became until eventually, I snatched him up and yelled at his ass. I became the bad guy after that, so I sat across the yard and got high and drunk by my-damn-self while everyone else enjoyed the party. Now it was basically over, and everyone had left but Stunna, Baby Jo, and Raheem. The kids were inside asleep, and the three of them were laughing and talking about Stunna proposing to Baby Jo while they cleaned up.

"Stupid motherfuckers. Look at 'em," I said, taking a swig of my beer as I watched them.

The longer I stared, the angrier I got. It must've been nice not to have a fucking thing to worry about. I bet it felt real good not to have grief tugging at your fucking heart and plaguing your mind every single minute of the day. No one knew what I was going through. No one knew what it was like to sit at the crib in the exact same spot my daughter lost her life in for hours.

I beat myself up over and over again thinking about that shit. If only I'd gotten off the phone sooner, I would've been able to see she was choking and helped her before it was too late. Or maybe if I hadn't taken that phone call at all, or if I'd just been paying more attention to her, I could've stopped it. I constantly thought of what I could've done differently, but at the end of the night, it didn't matter, because I couldn't bring her back. Now I was fucking up with my son, and it was obvious he needed me. He needed a man in his life, and I'd abandoned him because I was trying to teach Munchie a lesson. I was fed the fuck up with a lot of shit, and I allowed the rage to overtake me.

"Don't nobody giva fuck 'bout me!" I yelled and threw my beer bottle across the yard, almost hitting Baby Jo with it.

"What the fuck!" she yelled and looked in my direction as I staggered toward them.

"All y'all dead to me! I don't ever wanna see y'all fucking faces again! Ain't nobody here for me! Y'all don't giva fuck 'bout my daughter! Y'all out here laughing and shit, having a good ol' time like my daughter not six feet under! She gone! She dead! And y'all expect me to sit up here and celebrate? I'm da nigga that's done been there for you motherfuckers at least once, if not multiple times, but what about me?" I yelled, banging on my chest as warm tears started to roll down my face. "I can't take this shit no more!" I hollered and then started tearing down the fucking decorations. "Fuck a party! Fuck life!" I yelled, grabbing a blue cooler still full of ice and drinks and throwing it across the yard too.

"Bruh, you drunk. Come on. Let's get ready to go," Raheem said, walking over to grab me but I pushed his ass.

"Getcho gah damn hands off me, nigga."

"Bishop, please calm down," Munchie said, coming over to step in between us.

"What? You his bitch? Huh! You steppin' in for this nigga? Man, fuck this nigga," I said, pushing her forehead back with my index finger.

"Dawg, just relax," Stunna said, and Baby Jo pulled him back like she didn't want him getting involved.

"Y'all fucking?" I questioned, looking from Munchie to Raheem. "I should blow yo' brains out." I pointed at Rah. "I should fucking kill you." I swung on him, and Munchie moved out the way just in time before we started going blow for blow. Stunna ran over and started trying to to pull me back.

"Y'all, stop this shit! Cut it the fuck out," Munchie said, trying to intervene again, but one of our fists connected with her face and knocked her on her ass. I wasn't sure what happened after that, because everything went black.

12

MUNCHIE

"Munch, you sure you good?" Baby Jo asked as we stood in the kitchen and I nodded.

"Yeah, girl, I'm fine," I said, placing the ice pack I'd been holding on my face down on the counter.

I couldn't believe Bishop and Raheem started fighting. Raheem knew Bishop's ass was drunk, so I didn't even know why he entertained him, especially not after Bishop did the absolute most and yelled in BJ's face. I spazzed the fuck out because it wasn't necessary ,and he wasn't about to be taking his damn anger out on my son. Yeah, BJ was bad, but he was definitely just being a typical one-year-old. Bishop would've known that if he hadn't missed the last nine months of his fucking life.

I knew it was going to be some shit when he started looking spaced out with this weird ass grin on his face. He'd been watching us for a while and drinking shot after shot with I didn't know how many beers. I thought maybe once he'd gotten drunk he would be ready to go home and crash, but nope. That didn't happen. His drunk ass punched me in the face when I was trying to break up the fight. I didn't think he did it on purpose, but I was over everything. Yet I still felt real bad for him because I could only imagine what he was going through.

"You sure?" she asked, grabbing my chin to inspect my face, and I pushed her hand away.

"Yes. I'm just over this whole entire night."

"Munchie, what the hell has been going on here?" she questioned, and I sighed.

"Nothing. This is my first time seeing Bishop since the funeral. I knew he'd been having a tough time because Rah told me he's been reckless out in the streets and that he can't talk to him. And honestly, I don't know how to help either," I said, going to take a seat at the kitchen table.

"The damage is done, and at this point, y'all going to be better off coming clean and going from there. It's going to hurt him, but I think he'll be able to deal with it better if y'all tell him the truth instead of letting him find out another way." Jody came and stood at the table.

"How would he find out another way? I can't tell him shit. He's already lost his daughter, Jody. Are you not fucking thinking?" I asked, looking at her crazy.

"My bad. I'm just trying to put an end to this madness before it ends another way."

"It's not!" I snapped, and she tossed her hands up in the air and shook her head.

"Fine. Do it your way, but I've told you a million times ain't no easy way out of this shit. It doesn't matter how long y'all try to come up wit' a plan or figure shit out. This mess ain't ending in no fairy tale, so stop lying to yourself," she said sternly, and I took a deep breath.

"You're right. Trust me, I know, but don't worry about me. We have a wedding to start planning." I smiled, and she relaxed her face.

"How 'bout I take BJ with me for the night? I know you're exhausted, and I'll bring him back in the morning before we go to the airport," she offered.

"Yeah, that sounds good. Thank you." I wasn't even surprised she was going back to Vegas, and I didn't blame her.

"You don't have to thank me. I'm here for you. I just feel like you're making shit worse for yourself. But I'll let you handle it your own way," she said and leaned down to give me a hug. She really was right, but I honestly didn't know what to do anymore. I got up and followed her out of the kitchen to help get the kids to their car. Once she and Stunna were pulling off, I walked back into the kitchen and found Raheem sipping from a bottle of water.

"So what we gon' do 'bout him?" he asked, looking toward the living room where Bishop was sprawled out on the couch. After Bishop hit me, Raheem knocked him the hell out and had Stunna help move Bishop to the couch, where he was fast asleep.

"Just let him stay here for the night," I sighed.

"I don't know 'bout that shit, Munchie."

"Rah, don't," I warned, looking over at Bishop.

"Don't what? Let that nigga stay in the same house as you so he can do who knows what when he gets up? Man, nah. He ain't staying here. And shit getting real fucked up, Munchie. BJ almost blew our damn cover earlier."

"How?"

"Man, BJ know that nigga ain't his fucking daddy. He came running right to me yelling my name. Do you know how bad it fucks wit' me to keep having to act like that ain't my son?"

"Would you shut da fuck up," I hissed, peeking over at Bishop.

"That nigga can't hear us. You hear how loud he snoring? He knocked the fuck out." Raheem waved Bishop off.

"Yeah, but still. I don't want to take any chances. Use ya damn brain," I fussed.

"What you want him to stay here for, Munchie?" Raheem questioned, ignoring what I'd said.

"Because he obviously needs some-fucking-body."

"It ain't gotta be you," he countered.

"Then who, Rah? You saw the episode he had outside, and you still knocked him out cold. That was real fucked up."

"So I was just 'posed to let that nigga rock yo' shit? Do you see yo' face?" He frowned, and I rolled my eyes.

"He didn't do it on purpose. I stepped in the damn way. He's grieving right now, and that's more important than any of this shit." I waved my hands in the air.

"Yeah, you sure that's all it is? Be real." Raheem studied my face.

"That's all it is. Listen, can you just leave? I'm ready to go to bed. The whole left side of my face is swollen, and I don't want to argue. I'll call you first thing in the morning, and you can come pick him up yourself, but he needs to rest tonight and sleep that shit off," I reasoned.

"Walk me to the door," Raheem said reluctantly like he knew Bishop staying over wasn't a good idea. I walked him to the door, and then we stepped out on the porch.

"I love you," I told him, squeezing his hand.

"Yeah," he said and then walked off the porch. I stood there shocked for a minute as I watched him get in his car and pull off. I guess he had an attitude, but I had too much on my plate to deal with. I went back inside and locked the door, and when I walked in the living room, my heart skipped a beat. Bishop was sitting up on the couch and looking straight at me.

"Shit. You scared me," I said, grabbing my chest.

"What da fuck happened?" he asked, looking around like he was confused as he held on to the side of his head.

"You don't remember?" I questioned.

"Nah. Where er'body at?" he asked, looking around, and I didn't know if I believed him.

"Baby Jo and Stunna left a few minutes ago and took BJ with them."

"Rah?"

"He just left too. You don't remember y'all gettin' into it?" I crossed my arms over my chest.

"Not really. I'm all fucked up, Munchie." He shook his head, and I saw the sadness all in his eyes for the first time. I swallowed hard before speaking.

"Yeah, I figured that much. Just try to sleep it off," I suggested, turning on my heels and getting ready to head up the stairs.

"Can we talk?" he asked, stopping me in my tracks, and I turned back around to face him.

"Can it wait until morning?"

"No!" he yelled, scaring me a little bit. "Munchie, please," he said calmer. "I need you right now." I sighed before walking over and taking a seat next to him on the couch. "What happened to yo' face?"

"That's not important at the moment," I said, and either he'd gotten so drunk he couldn't remember shit, or Raheem really knocked the fucking memory out his head. "What's on your mind?" I finally asked. Only I would still try to help and be there for him after the shit he'd said to me earlier.

"I've blamed you for what happened to my daughter. I blamed you for leaving, and I blamed anything and anyone else for what happened. But I know I don't have anyone to blame but myself, and that shit fucking with me bad. I finally got over that shit wit' my parents, and now it's something all over again. I can't keep a female in my life for shit. First, I lost my mother. Then I had to deal with my sister not fucking wit' a nigga. After that, I lost you, and after you went my daughter. What da hell is wrong wit' me? Why me, Munch? And maybe I deserve it, but my daughter didn't!" he yelled, and tears ran down my face as I wrapped my arms around him. The hurt in his voice was chilling.

I felt like shit because I knew the things he'd battled with in the past. I knew how fucked up he was on the inside, and I promised myself I would heal him. Instead, I hadn't done shit but hurt him even more. And yeah, he cheated on me, but I'd betrayed him in a way that couldn't be undone. I'd crossed a line that should've never been touched, and I felt like a horrible person because of it.

"Fuck, man," Bishop said, trying to get himself together as he cried with his face buried in my neck.

"It's okay. Let it out... Let it all out," I said soothingly as I rubbed his back.

"I'm sorry about this," he said, and I shushed him.

"Don't be. You need this."

The room fell silent with nothing but the sounds of Bishop crying. His anger was one thing, but seeing him this hurt was completely different. For the first time, his pain was on full display, and I didn't know how to take it. My mind was all over the place, and I hated he was going through so much grief. There was no telling how long he'd been holding this shit in, and maybe coming to BJ's birthday party wasn't the best idea after all. It was too much for him too soon, and I hated I failed to realize that.

It was an hour later before Bishop finally fell asleep on my shoulder. I allowed him to lay there for another thirty minutes before shaking him and telling him to stretch out on the couch because I was going to bed. Once I stood up, he stretched out, and I went to grab him a blanket and pillow out the hallway closet. Then I came back and stuck the pillow under his head before covering him with the blanket and going upstairs to my bedroom. As soon as I walked in there, I stripped out of my clothes and went the master bathroom that was connected.

I turned mostly hot water on in the shower, stepped inside, and closed my eyes as the water fell down on me. I just stood there for twenty minutes before finally washing myself repeatedly until eventually I rinsed off and got out. I was so tired I quickly dried off and went to climb straight in my bed, and it was like I fell asleep as soon as my head touched the pillow.

"Who's that?" I asked as my eyes popped open. I wasn't sure how long I'd been sleeping, but I heard my door opening. Then the door closed, and I saw a figure moving toward my bed.

"It's me," Bishop said, pulling the covers off my body.

"What are you doin'?" I questioned, trying to hide myself with my hands, even though the room was mostly dark. He got in the bed with me, and I quickly realized he didn't have on anything but his underwear. "Bishop, no," I said as he lay on top of me and pulled the covers over us. He smelled like a damn liquor barrel.

"Please, Munch. Don't tell a nigga no right now. I need you," he whispered, then started kissing on my neck, and his fingers found my nipple that was rock hard.

"We can't."

"Why? You fuckin' somebody else?" he asked with an attitude, stopping what he was doing.

"No, I'm not. I just don't think we should be doing this right now with your feelings all over the place," I explained, not daring to say the real reason why.

"I know what I want. You still my wife, and I need you. Please, help a nigga feel a little better. I ain't had none in so long," he said like he was out of breath, then I felt him reach down and pull his dick out of his boxers.

He covered my mouth with his and wasted no time sliding his dick in my pussy with force, and it wasn't long before my body relaxed and my pussy got wet for him. My legs immediately wrapped around his waist, and he dug into me like he never had before. Less than two minutes later, he nutted all inside me. Then he rolled on his side and fell asleep, and once I came down from the high I was on, I instantly regretted my decision.

And only a few weeks later did I find out I was pregnant again.

❧ 13 ❧

RAHEEM
A COUPLE MONTHS LATER

"You playing wit' me. Tell me you fucking playing wit' me!" I yelled, looking down at Munchie as she sat on my couch.

"I wish I was, but I'm not," she said, dropping her head.

"What da fuck was you thinking! I asked you if anything happened between you and that nigga when he stayed at your house, and you said no. Now you tellin' me you pregnant wit' his muthafuckin' baby? Munchie what da fuck!" I yelled, trying to keep my cool, but I was livid.

"Just calm down."

"How the fuck I'ma calm down, bruh? How you gon' get away from the nigga now when you done went and got pregnant by him? Matter fact, how you know the baby not mine?" I asked, pacing the floor.

"We didn't have sex at all that month, Rah, cuz you and Bishop was on the road a lot, remember? I just slipped up that night after BJ's party, and that's the only time I had sex that whole month, so you do the math."

"Fuck!"

How crazy was that shit? My mind didn't fool me, and I knew I should've woke Bishop up and took his ass home. But I trusted

68

Munchie when she said she was going to let him sleep that shit off and then call me the first thing the next morning. She ended up not calling me at all, and when I hit her up she said she'd taken him home herself. When I asked her what happened, she said that Bishop was so drunk he didn't remember anything from the night before.

It sounded like a bunch of bullshit, but I didn't question it. The tables had turned on my ass, and I didn't know how to feel about it. I'd woke up in a good mood this morning until Munchie pulled up with some bullshit. I should've known it was coming because she'd been real moody over the last couple of months, and Bishop had gone back to his normal self.

He wasn't acting reckless anymore, and he was real relaxed about a lot of shit. That was a sudden change, but I figured maybe Munchie had talked some sense into the nigga. What I didn't expect was her fucking and keeping in touch with him. I mean, I knew I couldn't tell her she couldn't talk to him, because she was still married to him. Shit was all fucked up, and I was starting to realize how Bishop would feel if the truth got out about me and Munchie. The shoe was on the other foot, and that shit didn't feel good, but what the fuck could I do? I plopped down on the couch and just looked at Munchie.

"I'm so sorry. I felt bad for him. I really did, and I slipped up," she sighed.

"How long have you known you was pregnant, Munchie?" I questioned because it was my first time hearing about any of that shit.

"I found out a few weeks after we had sex and I didn't get my period."

"So you been knowing this shit and didn't think to tell me not once? You lied to my fuckin' face."

"Rah, I didn't know what to do."

"So that's all I'ma ever be good for? Helping you figure shit out even when you cross me?"

"I crossed him first though."

"And he crossed you before that. What the hell does it matter now? You backtracked, and that shit just fucked up everything."

"But it doesn't have to. I still love you. Bishop's not who I want. You know that," she pleaded, and I glared at her.

"I don't know shit no more."

"Rah," she said, sliding closer to me on the couch and grabbing my hand. "Let's just pack our shit and leave, okay?"

"Does he know you're pregnant? And don't lie to me." She dropped her head again, and that was my answer. "So you told him?" I asked just to clarify.

"I had to. He was so upset about losing Bella, and I thought the news would help him," she admitted. *Stupid.*

Well, that explained why Bishop had been so fucking calm. He had another baby on the way, and that probably gave him hope and helped with his grief in some type of way. Everything was starting to make a lot of damn sense, and to think, I'd been telling myself I was tripping for the last couple of months. But maybe shit wasn't as bad as I thought.

"I got an idea," I finally said a few minutes later.

"You do?" Munchie asked, sounding surprised.

"I've made some connections of my own, and I got some things in the works with this guy overseas. Before I jumped up and did anything, I wanted to give shit time and make sure it would be beneficial for me."

"What are you talking 'bout?"

"Listen. The plan has always been to cut ties wit' Bishop ever since I found out BJ was mine. But when we walked away, that meant walking away from the drug game, so I had to get some other shit in order. I got this dude overseas that wanted to open up his own resort. All he needed was an investor, and that's where I came in at. But the shit isn't done being built, and I need to know it's going to be successful before I go moving us out of the country. And this shit might've just bought us some more time. As much as I don't like this idea, I think the shit could work. But that's only if you're heart is still with me," I said, studying her to see if I could pick up on any signs of hesitation.

"My heart will always be with you. I just had a moment of weakness. I promise that's all it was," she said, and I believed her.

Shit was never going to be easy for us, and I knew that from the very first time I slid my dick inside her. Our love story was different, and I wasn't about to give up on her. I knew how Munchie's heart was, and if she said she had a moment of weakness, then that was the truth. After all, she'd belonged to Bishop first, but if I wanted her to myself, there was some risks I had to be willing to take. Although I was hurt, we could still fix things and make them work in our favor. It was just going to take longer than I originally intended, but I loved her, and that made it worth it. If it was a time to back out of shit, the time would've been then, but she had my heart, and that shit made me a little more understanding than I probably should've been.

"Here's what I got in mind. You listening?"

"Yeah, tell me," she said, sounding hopeful.

"I need you to move back in wit' him."

"What!" she yelled, jumping up off the couch, and I grabbed her hand and pulled her back down.

"Listen."

"Fuck no. I'm not doin' that shit. I know I fucked up, but we both know that's crazy as hell, Rah."

"This whole gah damn relationship crazy, Munchie. I need you to move back in wit' that nigga and buy us some more time. I know Bishop, and as long as his baby is in your stomach, he's not about to let up on you. Ain't no need in being in a different house and raising suspicions. You see how that nigga already accused us of fucking at BJ's party. Then he up and said he forgot some shit like that? I'm not buying it, and if anything, that nigga is trying to get some dirt on you. If he gets ahead of us, either one of us can pop up dead any damn day now. So we gots to stay ahead of him. Move back in wit' that nigga and kill any suspicions he may secretly have. I wouldn't be sending you back to live wit' him if I didn't plan to get you out of the shit."

"You absolutely promise to get me out?" she asked a few minutes later, and I nodded.

"Trust me."

We'd already made a bunch of stupid decisions up until then, so what more could another one hurt?

BISHOP

LATER THAT NIGHT

"D on't stop. Suck that shit," I said with a hand full of hair as I pushed her head down on my dick forcefully. I was at the casino in my office, sitting behind my desk while I got sucked up.

Knock! Knock!

"Mr. King," a white guy said, pushing the door open before I told his ass to come in. I wasn't worried about him seeing me get my dick sucked, because the bitch was under my desk between my legs. But I'd told that man a thousand times not to just coming barging his ass in my shit. He was the manager at the casino, and he was damn good at his job, but sometimes he didn't follow instructions well.

"What da fuck! Take yo' nerdy ass back out that door and try that shit again," I barked, and he quickly stepped out and closed the door back. **Knock! Knock!** "Don't stop sucking it," I said when the girl tried to pull away. "Come in!" I yelled out.

"Sorry about that, sir. Someone is here to see you. Where you expecting anyone tonight? If not, I can tell them to leave," he said, pushing his glasses up on his face.

"Who is it?"

"I'm not sure. It's two big African American guys," he said, nervously.

"Yeah, send 'em in."

"Alrighty," he said and then turned on his heels and walked out of the office.

"Fuckin' Poindexter," I said as he closed the door behind him. "Ay, you gotta get up and get out." I slid my chair back away from my desk, and she got up and fixed her work uniform.

"Okay, you want me to come over after work?" she questioned, and I shook my head.

"Nah. Munchie wants to talk when I get off."

"Y'all getting back together?" she asked.

"Dula, don't question me. Take ya ass back to work," I said, standing up to fix my clothes and zip my pants.

Dula started working for me a couple of months ago when she got fired from the strip club. Apparently, she got fired because some dude tried to stick a beer bottle up her pussy while she was dancing. She ended the dance quick, went to her car and grabbed her gun, and then snuck it back inside before shoving it in his damn face. After that, they told her she had to go and couldn't come back because she didn't handle the situation correctly or some bullshit like that. Since I had the casino and we could use some more bottle girls for the club, I hired her on the spot.

It wasn't like I didn't know her, and I guess I could say we had somewhat been cool since the day I met her at the strip club. But of course when she made a move on me a while ago, I didn't try to turn her down. Dula was bad as fuck, and I didn't give a damn if she and Raheem fucked around or not. She was clearly a pass-around hoe, and I didn't have a problem with treating her like one.

"I'm just asking because you paid me to come to the grand opening and get back cool with her. Munchie was a good friend while we were locked up, and I had to stab her in the back for money. If the job is over, I did all that for nothing." She crossed her arms over her chest.

"She may have been a good friend to you, but you stopped being one to her as soon as you took my fuckin' money to get some dirt on her, and you ain't told me shit that was helpful yet. So regardless of what we got goin' on, your services are no longer needed. I'll figure shit out my own."

"Whatever. I needed fuckin' money to survive out here. I was staying at my sister's and stripping every night, and it still wasn't enough to get me a nice place of my own after helping her out every fucking month. So I took the money and did what I needed to do, and yeah, Munchie and I have gotten close, but I was still doin' my job and trying to get dirt on her for you!"

"Well, she must didn't trust you after all."

"Or she hasn't been doing anything this whole time."

"Dula, stop acting like you give a fuck about her when we both know you don't. Now, get da fuck out my office and get back to work." I pointed at the door.

"Fine, but I want a fucking raise," she said and then strutted out the door as two guys walked in.

"What's up? Y'all can take a seat," I said and plopped back down in my chair before I cracked my knuckles.

The shit I was doing with Dula was the reason I wasn't tripping off Munchie when she moved out. I knew she wouldn't talk to me and keep me informed like I needed to be because obviously, she was trying to get the hell away from my ass. So the only way for me to know what was truly going on was to get someone to basically spy on her. And who was better than an old friend she wanted to rekindle a friendship with? I'd called Dula up the same day Munchie told me she was moving out. The shit was the smartest thing I'd ever did, but it hadn't paid off like I thought it would.

I just knew someone put Munchie up in that house, but after discovering she had a separate account that she'd been wiring money to from mine, it all made sense. And maybe she just needed time to herself after all because now she was pregnant with my baby. That wasn't part of my plan, but I really did miss her when I climbed in her bed that night. Things had been different with us since, and I allowed her to be there for me. Since she stayed in contact, I didn't force her to move back home, and I was trying to play my cards just right.

The fact that she wanted to talk to me after I got off told me that shit was on the right track. It was what I needed to get myself together again because before that night with Munchie, I had been slowly crashing out and that's why I had two big motherfuckers in my office now. Raheem missed work today, but he told me he would show up tonight. Yet his ass was nowhere to be found.

"What da word is?" I finally looked at the duo and asked.

"That nigga Leto you killed came for an organization called CC. Apparently, that stands for Cocaine Cartel, and that shit date back to the seventies. That's his blood family, but he was cut off when he started using the supply for his personal use. Instead of killing him, they tossed him out the cartel with no money or family to rely on, which is why he ended up coming to you to be supplied. The drugs weren't stolen. He didn't know who he was fucking with and decided to lie to you because it was his only way to get his hands on some good shit. So, turns out, you didn't kill him for nothing, but now his family has been informed about him being missing for the last few months. They got money, so they gon' get the answers they need one way or another. Our advice to you is to handle them before they come looking for you because trust me, they're going to come," one of them informed me, and I just sat there quiet for a minute.

I knew something was wrong with that dude, but I still chose to fuck with and supply him. He was talking numbers and carrying on like he knew the game in and out. Turned out, he did, but he'd been banished from his own damn family. Had I known that, I would've never gotten involved with his ass. When it came time to pay, he hit me with some bullshit ass lie about my money, so I killed him and didn't think twice about it. Then I saw some shit on the news about him being reported missing, so I had my people look into some shit, and they were just now getting back to me with the information I needed.

"I appreciate it," I said, sliding back in my chair. I reached in my pocket and grabbed a key out, and then I unlocked my bottom drawer that was filled with stacks of money. I pulled a few stacks out and placed them on my desk. "Keep me posted if anything changes, but I got it from here," I said, sliding the money over to them.

They snatched it up and placed it inside their jackets before leaving out of my office. As soon as my door closed, I tossed my head back and wondered what the fuck I was going to do next. After my plug started falling short with my supply, I'd gotten a new one just a couple of weeks before I killed Leto. Turned out, that new connect was his motherfucking family.

✤ 15 ✤

MUNCHIE
ONE MONTH LATER

"**D**amn, you look good," Raheem said as I walked up to the table he was at and placed BJ in the high chair.

"Thank you." I settled in my seat and pushed a strand of hair behind my ear.

I'd just left the hair salon, and the stylist installed a thirty-inch lace front for me. The hair was straight and jet black with highlights and a middle part. It was simple, and she'd done such an excellent job the hair actually looked like it was coming from my scalp. I'd never gotten my hair done by her before, but Bishop found her shop online and set up the appointment for me. She was expensive, and she had me feeling like a whole new person as soon as I walked out of there.

"You welcome," he said, leaning over to kiss me before turning and talking to BJ about nothing in particular.

When Raheem suggested I move back in with Bishop a month ago, I thought he was crazy. The plan sounded like the dumbest shit I ever heard, and I'd done and heard some dumb shit in my life. I just didn't see the point in it, but when he broke things down for me about his plan, it all made sense. Plus, I wanted to make our situation work and give us a chance to get out of the mess we'd created.

I moped around for weeks after having sex with Bishop because I knew I fucked up. It was so much that happened that night, and I just wasn't in the right headspace. Seeing Bishop flip out like that really did something to me. When he cried about his daughter, my judgment clouded up, and it had me pushing the disrespect to the side. I turned into that same girl who wanted to warm his heart and just make him feel better because I could only imagine what he was going through.

I didn't want to tell him no, so I gave in without much of a fight or thought about what that would mean for our future or even what it would make him think it meant. I still cared about Bishop, and I still had love for him, but that wasn't where my heart was anymore. I didn't have any confusion about who I wanted to be with, but that night helped me realize it definitely wasn't him. And it wasn't even because I thought he'd changed, but I was no longer the same person from when I first fell in love with him. I was a completely different woman, and Raheem understood that and respected it from the minute I got out of jail.

Anyway, when I found out I was pregnant, I broke down. It was at that moment I was able to understand how Baby Jo felt when she learned she was pregnant by T-Bank. It was like I felt trapped and didn't know how I would ever be able to get out of the situation. By then, I knew that a baby changed everything, and being that I didn't actually want to be with Bishop, it crushed me. Along with that came the bad nerves about how I would tell Raheem,

especially since I'd lied about not having sex with Bishop.

I was scared Raheem wouldn't want shit to do with me after that. Honestly, he would've had the right because the decision I made was stupid. It didn't matter what I told myself the reason for it was. I knew better, and I still did it after everything we had going on and everything we were fighting against just to be together.

Luckily, Raheem was a lot more understanding about shit

than I ever thought he would be. Of course he was pissed when he first found out, but he didn't resort to violence or making me feel like less of a human because of a mistake. He sat down and figured out a way for us to use the situation we were in to our own benefit. And if I ever had doubt that he really loved me, I didn't after that day. He wanted us to work out just as bad as I did, and he'd been taking actions to try to get us to that point.

That spoke volumes for me, and he had my full trust. I could rely on him to always be there, and it was appreciated, and so was he. The shit between us wasn't about getting back at Bishop but simply about following our hearts that led us to one another. Even if it had been a fucked-up ride, we would eventually get to our destination, and I truly believed that. We just had to take a damn detour, but it would be okay. Once the server walked over, I ordered drinks for me and BJ since Raheem was already sipping on something.

"Man, you funny just like yo' daddy," Raheem said to BJ, and that was when I realized he was holding a whole conversation with a toddler. I smiled and shook my head.

"You swear you understand what he saying." I laughed.

"I do. Stop hating."

"Whatever. Have you already ordered your food?"

"Nah, I was waiting on y'all. So what time you and Bishop going out tonight?" he questioned, and I sighed.

Unfortunately, it was my four-year wedding anniversary with Bishop, and the shit seemed to pop up quickly every single year. I dreaded it, and I cursed myself out for sleeping with him after I'd already gotten free of him. Now I was right back to the fake ass charade I had to put on with him. Surprisingly, things hadn't been so bad this time around. When I told Bishop I wanted to move back in, he was ecstatic and quick to make that shit happen.

We both agreed to take our time with things and give each other the space we needed. He stayed true to his word, and I honestly felt like he was just happy to have someone back in the house with him. We weren't sleeping together, and my excuse for that was needing a bed to myself. I told him my pregnancy was different that time around, and my body ached so much most nights that I couldn't even rest. I claimed I didn't want to keep him up and wanted to be able to relax in my own space without worrying or disturbing him.

He told me it wouldn't, but I insisted that I slept in one of the guest rooms. To my surprise, he agreed, and it seemed weird at first, but I accepted it and didn't think too much about it after that. So things had been great between us in a friendly way... as crazy as that sounded. But that friendly shit went out the window when he woke me up for breakfast in bed and told me happy anniversary. I found out he scheduled me a hair appointment and had plans for us that night, so I got up and got ready for the day and got BJ ready before heading out.

After I finished getting my hair done, I texted Raheem and asked if he wanted to meet us for lunch. He agreed, and we came to our favorite restaurant, which was only our favorite because it was ducked off and never too crowded. With the situation we had going on, we could use the privacy. I wanted to meet up with him to see how he felt about Bishop taking me out for our anniversary. It wasn't funny, but then again, it kind of was.

I was asking my side nigga for permission to go out with my husband, even though my side nigga had become my main nigga, and my husband was more like my side nigga. Fuck it. I couldn't even keep up with the shit anymore. I knew where my heart was at, and that was all that mattered. I still shook my head at myself though because four years ago, I would've never pictured things playing out the way they had... most definitely not with the way shit started for Raheem and me. I couldn't stand his ass for the longest, and he couldn't stand me, but there we were, two fools in love, and I did mean fools. We both knew the type of guy Bishop was and still risked it all.

"I think at seven or eight. Are you okay with this? How does it make you feel?" I questioned like I was his therapist. I needed to know though because I'd already hurt him, and I didn't want to do that again. Before he could respond, the server came back over and placed our drinks down. We quickly told her our orders, and then she walked away.

"Munchie, you already know how I feel about the shit. I don't like it, but it's part of the plan. What's da motto?" he asked, and I smirked at him.

"Fake it 'til you make it."

"And don't you forget it. You just make sure you not givin' that nigga no more pussy."

"Trust me. I'm not going down that road anymore. Does this shit ever get weird to you?" I questioned, picking up BJ's cup to help him take a sip. He was surprisingly pretty calm, and I figured it was because he took a nap on my lap while I was getting my hair done. Lord knew if he missed it, he would be like the Tasmanian devil.

"We been past the weird stage. This shit straight-up chaotic at this point." He laughed, and I was glad we were often able to make light of the situation.

"Do you know how much you have to love me to continue with this shit?"

"Baby, the question is if you know. The fuck?" he asked, and I laughed.

"Yeah, I know," I said, grabbing his hand.

"You still scared about the results of all this?"

"Sometimes," I admitted.

"Don't be, a'ight?"

"Okay," I agreed, and he leaned over to kiss me again. When the food finally came out, we got lost in our thoughts as we ate, and I couldn't help but feel like shit was going too good for it to stay that way.

16

BABY JO

"So when are we going shopping for this wedding dress?" Mary, Stunna's mother, asked. She was sitting on the couch across from me while I braided Ajay's hair, and Sunny stood in front of her with an iPad.

"No, Sunny. I don't want that," Ajay said as Sunny continuously tried to give her the iPad.

"Huhhh," Sunny said, not giving up.

"Sunny pooh, go show Miss Mary. Ajay don't want it," I said, turning Ajay's head to the side so I could catch up her hair.

"Ouu, yeah, let me take a look," Mary said, holding her hand out, and Sunny went running over to her so she could show her the game she had pulled up.

"We've already been shopping for it." I laughed, finally answering her question.

"Yeah, but you ain't found one you was even close to liking yet." Mary was more excited about this wedding than me, and that said a lot because I was over the damn moon about it. I was just being picky as hell when it came to my dress.

"So! My daddy can wait. Ain't that right, Mommy Jo?" Ajay asked, turning her head around to look at me.

"That's right, boo. Now turn yo' lil' head back around," I playfully fussed, tapping her on the nose.

It was hard to believe how big she was getting. She might've lost her little attitude with me, but she was still jazzier than ever with her mouth. Sometimes it was funny, and sometimes I couldn't do anything but shake my head. She had enough personality for a grown woman and started calling me "Mommy Jo" out the blue when we returned home from Vegas after BJ's birthday party.

Apparently, she'd told my mother that she wanted to call me mommy like Sunny did, and my mother suggested she call me Mommy Jo instead. We didn't learn that until we asked Ajay where she got the name. Although Stunna and I didn't explain our situation to anyone, we did explain it to Ajay so she could understand why my mother told her to call me that instead of just mommy. Even though her biological mother wasn't shit, that still wasn't a boundary I wanted to overstep. Just because her mama wasn't around or there for her didn't mean she wouldn't eventually come to her senses and want to build a relationship with her. However, Stunna and I did agree that it was okay for her to continue calling me that, and I wasn't going to lie; I loved it.

"And you stay out of grown folks' conversation, girl," Mary fussed, and Ajay smiled at her.

"I have ears, Granny. I can hear," Ajay said like that was her excuse to jump in the conversation.

"And you gon' be able to feel in a minute when I tap those little legs up. Spare the rod, spoil the child. Don't play wit' me." Mary pointed, and I had to laugh at that. Anytime she wanted to make a point, she used a scripture to back it up.

For the first time ever, I finally had a relationship with the mother of the guy I was talking to, although Stunna was my fiancé now. It was different though, because for years I hated T-Bank's mother. I didn't know how to have a good relationship with that woman, and she didn't want one with me. She never looked at me like family ,because I was always just the bitch from Miami that her son rescued.

She didn't even consider me to be his damn girlfriend most of the time. It was so much animosity between us that I eventually started to believe it was natural to beef with a nigga's mama. I didn't know any better, and she sure as hell didn't teach me any different. Everything was the complete opposite with Mary, and she'd accepted me from day one, even with all the drama Stunna and I had going on at that time. Mary was an angel, and I enjoyed building a strong relationship between us. It made me feel better and like I was doing something right.

"I'm just playing, Granny," Ajay said and switched her tone. She knew Mary didn't play. Stunna and I were a lot more chill and patient when it came to the girls though.

"Mhm." Marry nodded and shot Ajay a warning smile.

"What y'all talkin' 'bout in here?" Stunna asked, walking into the spacious living room. He was dressed in a red and white Givenchy jumpsuit that matched the one I had on while the girls wore these pink and black outfits that matched the beads I was putting in their heads. They loved to dressed alike, and I wondered how long that would last.

"You." Mary smiled as he walked over to give her a hug and kiss on the cheek.

"What's up, old lady?" He smirked, and she playfully punched him.

"Wisdom belongs to the aged, and understanding to the old."

"That's a fact. When you got over here?" he asked because he'd just got back home.

"I been here for about an hour now. Where you been?"

"Running errands and handling business like a real boss do." He cheesed, plopping down on the couch next to her. "What's up, Sunlight," he questioned as he lifted Sunny in the air above his head. I'd already finished her hair, and I was glad because Stunna returned quicker than I thought he would.

"Daddy, her name Sunny." Ajay laughed.

"And yo' name applejacks," he teased her.

"Nuh uhhh!" she squealed, and I grinned at them.

"Now back to this wedding dress." Mary cleared her throat.

"Ah shoot," Stunna laughed. He never cursed around his mama because she simply wasn't having it. It didn't matter how old he was. "Baby, what's going on wit' the dress?" He looked across the room at me.

"I can't decide on one, and I kind of wanted Munchie to help me pick one out."

"See, Ma? She on it." He laughed because he knew Mary was very invested in the wedding. I appreciated it though, because she could have been telling him not to marry me, yet she was all for it.

I finally finished Ajay's hair, and then Stunna got up to put her and Sunny's shoes on while I went upstairs to wash my hands. Thankfully, I thought to lay a towel across me while I braided the girls' hair so I wouldn't get any grease or anything on my clothes. We were going to the mall for a shopping spree on Stunna, and Mary had decided to come with us. She was going to be watching the girls for us later anyway because Stunna was taking me to a comedy show. It was one of our dates for the month, and I loved how he always switched shit up and tried to do something different every time.

Stunna was just as invested in me as he was in his business, and it didn't go unnoticed. The year couldn't go by quicker for me because I was ready to marry him. Stunna wasn't capping and giving me a ring just to stay engaged for forever. He actually wanted us to take that leap and enter the next chapter of our lives together. And maybe we were rushing things, but when you knew someone was for you, you just knew it. So there was no point and putting a certain pace on our love. It wasn't a sprint, but we damn sure was getting to the destination quickly. After I finished freshening up and running a comb through my silk-pressed hair, I went downstairs, and we all headed out for the day.

LATER THAT NIGHT

"We have to plan something for the girls," I said, sitting in the passenger's seat as Stunna drove in the direction of his mansion.

We'd just left from our comedy show, and I enjoyed myself, but I was tired as hell after shopping all day. I couldn't get home fast enough, and I was ready to lay under Stunna anyway since the girls wouldn't be coming back until the following morning. I figured they passed out and went to sleep hours ago because Ajay had us all over that mall, and Mary wasn't holding back either. It was nice to see a man cash out on his family, and we all enjoyed ourselves and grabbed a bite to eat before parting ways.

"What you got in mind? You know with Ajay in school, we gots to plan around her schedule."

"Yeah. I was thinking maybe we could take a trip for her spring break if you don't have to work," I suggested.

"That sounds good. Make the arrangements, and I'll clear my schedule for the dates."

"Bet." I smiled, and I couldn't wait to see where Ajay and Sunny was trying to go. Ajay was enrolled in a private school, and Stunna took her academics very seriously. That was another of those things that he didn't play about, and he even hired private teachers during the summer so she was constantly learning something, and it showed.

"Can I ask you something?" Stunna questioned about twenty minutes later.

"Duhhh, bae." I reached over to rub his arm as he drove. That was a crazy question.

"What happened wit' you and Bishop?" he asked, catching me off guard because we'd been joking around and talking about stupid shit before that.

"What you mean?" I cleared my throat, and he briefly looked at me.

"When I first met you y'all was tight as hell and he called you his sister."

"He still does," I pointed out.

"Yeah, but I've noticed the way things changed between y'all, and I've been wondering for a while what was going on there. I just never found the time to ask, but you always seem so tense when we go to Florida. I'on like that."

"Honestly, babe, it's a long ass story. Bishop and I were close, but after he cheated on Munchie with my cousin, things just went downhill from there. I didn't know it bothered you."

"I just want you to be happy, and if something is causing you stress, then it's my job to figure out what the hell it is and fix it."

"It's nothing. Bishop has just done a lot and made decisions that I didn't agree with."

"Like what?" he asked, making a turn at a light, and I sighed. I never really opened up to anyone about how I felt on a lot of things, but Stunna was going to be my husband, and I trusted that I could open up to him about the situation.

"I think he was the one who killed my cousin."

"The one he had the baby with? Why the hell would he do some fucked-up shit like that?" Stunna asked like he couldn't believe what I was saying.

"I know y'all have known each other for a while, but Bishop is more fucked up in the head than you might know. Something is really wrong with him. The nigga is very disturbed, and it's like I always knew it, but I never believed it until I started seeing shit for myself. I don't have proof that he killed her, but in my gut, I know it was him. Rissa had a way of being petty, and if she pushed the wrong buttons, I'm sure it set him off. But what was the point in going to the cops when I didn't have proof? And after everything he's done for me, that seemed like it was wrong. At the same time though, I feel like I'm wrong for not getting justice for her, but getting justice for her would've been like betraying Munchie. So yeah... Shit has been fucked up for a while, and I just ignore my emotions and keep my distance. And

I hate what happened to my little cousin Bella. That's why people need to be careful about how they do shit because you never know what the end result would be." I shrugged.

"Why you ain't been told me none of this, Jo? I'm over here thinking shit straight, and the whole time, your thoughts have been eating you alive. I'm here to make shit better for you, for us. You could've talked to me."

"I know," I said quietly, and he lifted my hand to his mouth to kiss it. "My life is confusing enough, and with you I had peace. So I didn't want to bring that disaster over into my peace, if you know what I mean."

"I get what you saying, but you have to be able to open up to me. And your feelings make sense. You're hurt over your cousin, but you feel the need to be loyal to them as well. So instead of picking a side, you chose distance. It ain't shit wrong with that decision, because you did what was best for you. Rissa is gone, and it seems like Bishop has already paid for that mistake in the worst way. Don't allow that stuff to fuck up your head, baby. You're human, and you've dealt with a lot. Everything don't always have to be solved, because sometimes you just have to let shit be, especially when there's nothing that can be done about it."

"I guess you're right," I said, letting his words marinate as he finally pulled up to the mansion.

"Who da fuck is this?" he asked, taking the words right out of my mouth.

"I don't know. It looks like a woman," I said as he parked. We both hopped out the car, and when we did the woman on his steps stood up. She had been sitting with her face buried between her knees.

"Marlon, where have you been!" she yelled, and I noticed her face was fucked up like someone used it as a damn punching bag. She had on baggy clothes and a hood was over her head, so I couldn't really make out much other than her fucked-up face.

"Amirah, what the hell goin' on?"

Oh, so he know the hoe?

"I need help. You have to help me. I can't go back there. Do you see what he did to my fucking face? I've been here for hours waiting on you! I tried to call your phone, but it said that number was no longer in service. You changed your number on me again? I have no one, and you know I don't. Is this how you treat the woman who gave birth to your daughter!"

Oh hell to the motherfucking no, no, no!

⚗ 17 ⚗

BISHOP

"Happy anniversary, baby," I said, clinking my wine glass with Munchie's sparkling water.

We were at a winery, and we'd been there for hours. We went on a tour of the place first, and then we tasted various kinds of wine for a while. Before I got too drunk, we went and learned about the process of everything before making our own bottles of wine. It cost me extra to do that because usually the winery only offered a tour and wine tasting. Since I wanted to make the day special, I paid the extra money, and it was worth it from the smile on Munchie's face. She couldn't drink, but she still seemed to enjoy the chill vibes.

We were out on the patio the place decorated for us. They were supposed to close about an hour ago, but since I paid to have the place to ourselves, they were willing to stay until we got ready to leave, and I'd even hired a chef to come out and cook us dinner. Originally, I didn't plan to overdo things since Munchie had only moved back in a month ago, and we was still working on things. Turned out, that was what she wanted to talk to me about that night when I got off work. I wasn't expecting to hear her say that, but when she did, I decided I was going to change shit up.

I couldn't expect better out of the relationship or her if I didn't stop my cheating and demeaning ways. I knew I needed her, but it was even more than I thought. Since I had her back, I wanted to really try things her way and give her what she asked for. My life fell completely apart when she left me, and I couldn't go through that shit no more. I couldn't do life without her by my side, and I was willing to do whatever to make sure I didn't have to.

I'd fucked up, and I was sure she'd fucked up too somewhere along the line. Too much time passed by for her not to. But since she was careful enough not to let that shit ever get back to me, I had to respect it. And I would respect it as long as she knew it was no longer acceptable. We agreed to work on things under the same roof for the sake of our kids, so that was what the fuck we was gon' do.

We had too much history to walk away from one another, and she knew too damn much. On top of that, I could never watch her with the next man, so us figuring it out was the safest thing to do. No one knew the things that crept inside my head often at the thought of my Munchie being with another nigga, and luckily they wouldn't have to. She was never leaving again, and I was willing to do my part to make sure she never wanted to.

"Happy anniversary, Bishop," she finally said and took a sip of her drink after just staring at me for a second. I couldn't tell what she was thinking, and it reminded me of when we first started talking, and I couldn't read her ass for shit. She was so damn weird to me at first. We'd come a long way since then.

"Did you enjoy yourself tonight?" I questioned, and she nodded.

"But who in the hell brings a pregnant woman to a winery?" she asked, and I busted out laughing.

"A'ight, so I ain't completely think shit through before I planned it. I was just trying to do something romantic for you. Today is a special day, and I wanted us to be somewhere off to ourselves and away from the bullshit. I needed to clear my head, and this seemed like the perfect place to do all that."

"I don't know... You never took me as the type to come to a winery." She raised her eyebrows.

"Well, I'm trying to do shit differently and show you that side of me you fell in love with. You don't miss the way things were in the beginning?" I questioned.

"It sure as hell was a lot peachier, or I was just naïve... One." She laughed a little, shrugging her shoulders.

"It was probably a lil' bit of both." I reached across the square glass table and grabbed both of her hands. "Where did we go wrong?" I asked, and she dropped her head for a second before looking back up at me.

"A lot of places, Bishop. Even the way we came into each other's life was fucked up."

"That might be true, but you don't think it was for a reason?"

"Yeah, I do," she said and looked away from me like her mind went somewhere else for a split second. I stared at her and then licked my lips.

"I need for us to work." I rubbed her hands with my thumbs as they rested in my palms. "I know I fucked up when I started messing with Rissa behind your back. You stayed solid when you could've folded on me, and that's the way I repaid you. It was grimy as hell when you was the best thing to happen to a nigga. I robbed you of the chance to have my first baby when that's all we talked about for those two years you was locked up. We had big ass plans, and I fucked us over. I was supposed to take you on a nice ass honeymoon and put a baby in you. Instead, I only took you to Vegas on a business trip because I knew I had a baby on the way. I wanted to tell you so many times, but I ended up convincing myself you was better off not knowing. You seemed so damn hopeful when you first got home, even after everything you'd been through, and I didn't want to take that away from you. I just..." I said, and my voice trailed off as I tried to figure out the right words to say.

"Bishop, we don't have to talk about this. It's in the past, and we've both moved on from it."

"Have we?" I questioned, and she just looked at me. "Because everything that happened after that was because we couldn't move on. We allowed that one situation to start a domino effect."

"No, that's what *you* allowed. And once the truth came out about Rissa, you started moving any kind of way. I told you I would stay, and you forgot my fucking worth right then and there. I didn't receive an ounce of respect from you after that."

"I gave you what you wanted." I frowned.

"But it wasn't what the fuck I needed, Bishop! Them streets couldn't love me. I only wanted you to do that, and you couldn't!" she yelled, almost sounding like she wanted to cry.

"I did love you and still do. I just fucked up. I fucked up. Never said I was perfect."

"You never said you was a cheater either," she mumbled, and my eyes lowered.

"Let me ask you something, Munch."

"I'm listening." She pulled her hands away from me and stuck one underneath her chin.

"Out of all this time... You never did shit?" I watched her closely, and she looked me dead in my eyes.

"Nope."

"Never?"

"No."

"Put that on our son." I glared at her and she swallowed hard.

"I'm not putting shit on my son."

"If you did, I promise you the time to tell me is now."

"I didn't. Can we go?" she asked, standing up fast, and then she hunched over and grabbed her side.

"You alright?" I asked, jumping up to check on her, and she nodded.

"I'm fine."

"You sure?" I questioned, and she nodded again as she stood

up straight. "Okay, let's get you home so you can lay down, and then I'll go pick up BJ from Baby Jo's mama's house. I don't want you taking that ride if you're in pain, and I didn't mean to upset you. If you say you never fucked around, I believe you, baby."

❧

Once I dropped Munchie off at home, I gave her, her present, which was a Cartier LOVE bracelet made out of white gold with colorless diamonds and BJ's name engraved on the inside along with the words *My Angel*. She loved the gift so much she started crying. It was a thoughtful gift, but I didn't think she would cry over it. Then again, she was pregnant and emotional, so I didn't give her a hard time. I was just glad she liked the gift. Things might've gotten a little heated before we left the winery, but it was a conversation we needed to have.

Now I was on my way to pick up BJ because Jody's mama had somewhere to be early in the morning. My phone was constantly ringing on the passenger's seat, but I turned my music up and ignored it. I thought about a lot of shit and everything I had been through, and I was more determined than ever to make shit work with Munchie. As long as she knew I was trying, that was all that mattered to me.

I finally made it to Baby Jo's mama's house about thirty minutes later and got out to go knock on the door. She asked who it was, and when I told her it was me, she pulled the door open. She stayed in a bad neighborhood, but she was known as the church lady who would give a stranger the shirt off her back. So no one really bothered her, and it was plenty dudes around that way that respected her and were looking out for her.

"Come on in, baby. He's asleep, so try not to wake him," she said, and I smiled as I walked through the door.

"I got you. You been alright?"

"Yep. I'm making it. I'm just glad I can spend time with BJ since my own granddaughter is barely in town," she said and laughed a little. "But I'm happy for Jody. She really has come along way. I figure Florida has too many bad memories for her though. It's never been a place she wanted to be."

"True," I said as she walked out the small living room, and a few seconds later she was walking back in with BJ asleep on her shoulder. I walked over and took him from her, and he laid his head on my shoulder and wrapped his arms around my neck.

"Alrighty. Y'all get home safe and let me know when you need me to watch him again."

"A'ight. Here you go," I said, digging in my pocket and pulling ten one-hundred dollar bills out.

"Lord, child, I can't take all that," she fussed like I knew she would.

"Take it and put what you don't want in the offering plate."

"Well, I'm not gon' argue with that," she said, taking the money and walking me to the front door.

"A'ight now. I'll see you," I said as I walked outside.

"Okay, baby." She closed the door, and I went to my car and strapped BJ in his car seat. Then I hopped in the driver's seat and started the car up before pulling off. As soon as I did, a car that had been sitting on the side of the road did a U-turn and got behind me.

❧ 18 ❧

MUNCHIE
A FEW DAYS LATER

"Baby. Baby, get up for me," a voice said, and then I felt someone shaking my leg.

"Go away!" I yelled, not wanting to be bothered.

"Munchie, it's Rah. Sit up for me," Raheem said and took a seat next to where my feet were on the bed. I slowly pulled the cover from over my head and sat up. My eyes were bloodshot red, and my bonnet was hanging off my head. I had on a huge T-shirt with stains all over it, and I didn't even give a fuck.

"What is it, Rah? Why are you here?" I questioned, and my voice was hoarse from crying out loud for the past few days.

I couldn't stop the tears from coming, and even as I looked at Raheem, they were rolling down my face, telling exactly how I felt. I thought my anniversary was ending decent for the most part when Bishop dropped me off at home and gave me my gift the other night. That was until I woke up the next morning and realized I was at the house alone. I was so tired I didn't even notice Bishop and BJ never made it back that night. I passed out, and when I woke up, I was confused as hell.

Right when I was about to call Bishop, he walked in the house and broke the fuck down. I didn't know what was going on, and I just kept asking him where BJ was, but he couldn't speak. All he did was cried and cried, and when he finally looked up at me, I knew something wrong. My suspicions were confirmed when he told me his car got shot up. I begged him to tell me that was before he got BJ, and when he told me it was right after, I lost it. I felt sick to my stomach, and I threw up right there.

It didn't seem right, and I just knew our luck couldn't have been that fucking bad. But when Bishop told me he had some shit going on with his plug after a killing a family member of his by accident, I knew our luck was indeed that motherfucking bad. Bishop was in my face all day long and all night, and not once did he mention he was having problems out in the streets. I knew I didn't want anything to do with the streets anymore, but I needed to know something like that. I couldn't fathom how he could be so damn stupid he didn't take any precautions.

Had I known some shit like that, I would've never even left the house with him, and he sure as hell wouldn't have been picking my son up from nowhere. Clearly, we had been followed that entire night, and I felt paranoid on the estate. I wanted to go back to my own house, but I could hardly even move over the last few days. When I found out I couldn't even see my son's body, I flipped out all over again. According to Bishop, the police didn't want anyone viewing the body until after they wrapped up their investigation or some crazy shit like that.

Then he got a phone call the next day asking what funeral home did we want to use. By then, I'd clocked out completely and allowed Bishop to oversee everything since he seemed to be handling shit way better than me, but I guess it was because he'd already been through the exact same situation before.

"Bishop is at the funeral home waiting. He sent me to get you," Raheem said, snapping me out of la-la land.

"You already saw his body?" I sniffed, and Raheem shook his head.

"Before I could go in, Bishop was coming out and telling me to come get you. He gave me his house keys to get in. Come on.

I'm not gon' be able to do this shit without you," he said in a faint voice.

"I just don't understand. Our baby is gone," I said before breaking down, and Raheem got up and wrapped his arms around me. "Why is this shit happening? What's going on?" I questioned as he kissed the side of my head. "Why wouldn't you tell me someone was after y'all?"

"Munchie, I ain't know. I'm just as fucked up as you are."

"You made me come back," I sobbed as snot dripped from my nose.

"I know, baby. I'ma figure it out. Just give me time."

"I already did!" I yelled in his face and then pushed him off me. I climbed out of the bed, walked into the bathroom, and then slammed the door closed and locked it. I placed my back against it and slid down to the floor. I wasn't sure how much time passed by before I finally got up and took my shower.

When I eventually emerged from the bathroom, I was naked with nothing but a bonnet on my head. I didn't see Raheem anywhere, and I figured he must've gone downstairs. I walked across the room and went into the closet to throw on anything. I didn't feel much better, but I was refreshed and ready to get to the funeral home. I'd cried all the tears I could in the shower, hoping that would help me keep myself together. I didn't mean to get upset with Raheem, because I knew he was going through it just like me. After grabbing a jacket and my purse, I walked out the room and went to find Raheem.

"I'm sorry," I said when I walked into the living room, and he stood up and walked to kiss me. That was his way of telling me it was okay before we left out.

Almost forty minutes later, we pulled up in front of the funeral home and got out of Raheem's car. We made sure to keep a small distance between us as we walked inside. As soon as we did, Baby Jo rushed over to hug me, and I squeezed her tightly. Although she and Stunna came to town as soon as they found out what happened, I hadn't seen them. I couldn't talk to anyone, and I stayed in my bedroom for days.

"Munchie, I'm so so sorry. I hate this shit happened to y'all. It's gon' be okay, boo. I'm here," she said, and I nodded as she stepped back. "Do you want to get some air?" she questioned, trying to pull me outside.

"No. I need to see my baby's face," I said, and she looked over her shoulder at Bishop and then at me with a worried expression on her face. "Munchie—" she said, and I cut her off.

"Where is the casket?" I asked, finally noticing that it wasn't one. I walked around Baby Jo and came face-to-face with Bishop, who was holding something in his hands. "What's goin' on?" I asked. "Where is he? Did they fuck something up!" I yelled because I was sick of the police, coroner, and whoever else that kept playing with us when it came to my son's body.

"Nah, he right here." Bishop shook his head, and I frowned.

"Right where!"

"Here," he said, holding out what he had in his hands.

"What da fuck is this? Bishop, I know damn well you didn't —" I started to say and then threw my hands up to my mouth as I realized what was really going on. "You bastard! You had my son cremated!" I yelled. He wasn't just holding some random item; it was an urn.

"You ain't wanna see him like that. Didn't nobody need to see him like that! I did what was best for us. He'll always be with us this way. I ain't want no funeral with everyone looking all at him and shit. Man, fuck no!" Bishop barked.

"That wasn't your decision to make!" I yelled and started hitting him wherever I could. "What da fuck is wrong witchu! Why would you do this! Why would you do this!" I yelled, and before I could fall out crying, I felt someone's arms wrapping around me body to keep me up.

"Get her out of here. Take her home," Raheem said, and I shook my head.

"Noooo! Get off me. Let me go! Where is my son? I want my

son!" I cried, completely flipping out. I was throwing my arms all around and trying to get Raheem off me while trying to hit Bishop in the mouth at the same damn time. I was a complete mess, and I had every reason to be.

"He gone, Munchie. He gone," Bishop kept saying, sending chills through my body.

19

BABY JO

A FEW MONTHS LATER

"I just don't understand how Bishop is so calm about this shit. It doesn't make sense, and then he just up and burned my baby's body without asking me a thing. How could he do something like that to me?" Munchie asked on the other side of the dressing room door.

We were out looking for me a wedding dress because I still hadn't found one. It was already April, and Stunna and I weren't able to take the girls on a trip for spring break because I'd been flying from Vegas to Florida often to be there for Munchie. The past few months had been hard as hell for her, and I felt awful that they were having to go through tragedy once again. Munchie had been hospitalized twice already because she wasn't eating like she needed to be while pregnant.

Depression was definitely getting the best of her, and I was surprised when she called and asked about us going dress shopping. But I was all for whatever would get her out of the house and take her mind off things for a few hours. Or at least that was what I thought I was doing, yet her mind hadn't left that situation not once, and it was all she was talking about. But if it helped her to vent, I was all for that too. She was going to be my matron of honor, and originally, Stunna wanted Raheem to be his best man. But knowing what I knew, I refused to let that happen and suggested he gave Bishop the title instead.

There was no point in giving Bishop a reason to flip out at our wedding all because he sensed what was going on with Munchie and Raheem. So that had been settled, and I'd told Munchie repeatedly to let me know if they weren't going to be able to do it. I didn't even feel right asking her for help or expecting her to show up after she lost her son. I'd contemplated pushing the wedding back until she was able to stand by my side because Munchie was like a sister to me. She was quick to shut that idea down and told me not to let what was going on with her slow down things for me.

Then she admitted it wouldn't be easy but that she would be there for me on my big day because I'd always been there for her. I just wanted her to get that same happiness and love in return without having to worry about anything. She deserved that too, regardless of the mistakes she'd made. Munchie had been through just as much as me, and I wanted us both to be happy, not just me. Now Raheem... That was a different story because what was the reason for his disloyalty? Bishop crossed Munchie, not him.

"Okay... I don't like that one," I said, finally walking out of the dressing room.

"I'll go grab a couple of more for you to try on," the nice white lady who'd been helping me try on the dresses said and then rushed away. I walked over to where Munchie was sitting in a plush cream-colored chair and took a seat in the one next to her.

"Maybe it's because he's been through this before, and he didn't want to go through the pain of burying another child," I reasoned, although I ended up jumping on Bishop at that damn funeral home.

The way Munchie broke down crushed me, and I wanted to kill him. He was wrong for what he did without consulting her first. It was fucked up, and what made it even worse was that BJ wasn't his son for him to make that decision at all. But with the way things was set up, no one could say a thing. I saw the look in Raheem's eyes, and I knew it took everything in him not to do what I did. Munchie and I ended up getting kicked out, and Stunna took us back to her house while Raheem was stuck with Bishop. In conclusion, shit was fucked up.

"I don't give a damn! It wasn't right."

"No, it wasn't, but that's the only thing that makes sense for why he did that shit."

"I should've never allowed him to handle the funeral arrangements, but I was so out of it, Jody."

"I know, babe. But what else was you supposed to do when he's your husband and he think he's BJ's father?"

"I don't know, but I can never forgive him for this," she said, and I nodded, understanding completely. I could only imagine how much of a slap to the face that was to Munchie after she'd just watched him spend over five hundred thousand on Bella's funeral. There was no comparison, of course, but it had to sting when he cremated BJ and stuck him up on the shelf like it was nothing. She never even got to see BJ one last time.

"I don't blame you."

"But how are things going for you back in Vegas?" she questioned, changing the subject as she looked over at me.

I knew she was asking about my situation with Stunna's baby mama, but there really wasn't much to talk about. She popped up that night and wanted Stunna to let her stay and see her daughter because she claimed she didn't have anywhere else to go. She was scared her boyfriend would find her and whoop her ass again. Stunna said he hated that happened to her, but she couldn't stay with us. That was when she actually noticed and asked who the hell I was.

Stunna introduced me as his fiancée, and she started going off about me not being her daughter's mother. The woman was delusional and bitter as hell. She wasn't happy, so she didn't want Stunna to be happy either, even though she was the one who chose not to be a mother and walked away from both of them. Being that she was getting beat on and I'd been through that before, I wanted to feel bad for her, but she made it hard. The things that came out of her mouth were unacceptable, and Stunna threatened to call the police if she didn't leave because he knew I was ready to beat her ass a second time.

"Nothing. We haven't heard anything from her since she left that night."

"Forget battle of the bands. You and Stunna are having the battle of the exes," she said, making me laugh as the woman walked back over with a few more dresses. She placed her hand on her six-month-pregnant belly, and I smiled at her.

"Girl, you crazy. Let me go try these on." I got up and went back to the dressing room, and about five minutes later, I stepped out with the dress on and Munchie's face lit up. "What about this?" I asked, holding my arms out.

"That's the one," she said, and I couldn't wait for my wedding day.

20

RAHEEM

"What the fuck is this place?" I asked as I parallel parked in front of a building.

"Nigga, you can't read? It's a coffee shop," Bishop said, looking out the window.

I couldn't stand being around the nigga. The shit was starting to mess with my head, and after he cremated my son, I really felt some type of way. I didn't give a fuck what the situation looked like. I was pissed the fuck off, and killing the nigga wasn't seeming like such a bad idea after all. He was hiding something from me, but I didn't know what.

I wasn't the best person to speak on that, because I was hiding shit from him as well. I just found it crazy as a bitch that we had beef with the whole motherfucking cartel, and the nigga didn't mention the shit to me once. Ever since BJ's birthday party, Bishop had been different. I assumed it was because he learned about Munchie being pregnant again, but that wasn't it. The look in his eyes was eerie, and it was crazy that we'd gotten to the point where I couldn't trust him, and he couldn't trust me either.

"What kind of cartel boss you know running a damn coffee shop?" I mugged him.

"How do you think he move his drugs from Mexico? You worried about the wrong shit. Let's go handle this business," he said, opening his car door after making sure his gun was on him.

We were all the way in California meeting with the cartel boss, aka our new plug. I'd been trying to get at the nigga ever since I found out he was the one responsible for BJ's death. Bishop kept putting it off, saying he couldn't focus on that shit after losing another child. Meanwhile, I couldn't sleep, because I'd lost my first child, and I wanted revenge. He didn't seem to want the same thing, and since he was still under the impression that BJ was his son, I couldn't understand why.

Then a few days ago, he pulled up at my crib and told me our plug wanted to see us. We'd only met with him face-to-face, and that was once. Usually, we met up with his right-hand man to get our supply. We'd found out that our old plug had been locked the fuck up. He knew the police were cracking down on him, and that was why our supply had started to lack.

Fortunately, we cut him off just in time, and since he was way bigger than us in the drug world, the feds that cracked down on him weren't worried about who he had connections with. They had who they wanted, and a few other people that were still close to him went down as well. So it was like we dodged one bullet and got hit by another one. It also came out that the dude who tried to rob Bishop at the storage units and got killed by Munchie was just trying to take over Bishop's shit. And that information came from someone who was close to him and looking for a payday.

Unfortunately, he didn't get it, because I ran down on his ass and pushed his wig back. He was a loose end that we didn't need, so I tied it. I couldn't get who I really wanted, so it felt good to take my frustrations out on somebody. Now the day I'd been waiting on was here, and we were finally meeting up with the motherfucker who had my son killed. It wasn't like I had shit else to do, because our supply had stopped months ago. That was probably one of the main reasons why Bishop was anxious to meet with the plug today.

My business with the plug was over though. I'd only gone to do one thing. I didn't know what Bishop's plan was or what he thought he was getting out of the link up other than revenge, but we were about to find out because it was too many things that didn't add up for me. Bishop was never the type to just sit and wait. It didn't matter what the situation was, yet he refused to make the first move on them.

"Nigga, is you coming or what?" Bishop finally asked, standing outside of the car.

"Fa sho," I said and jumped out and slammed my door shut. I patted my jeans to make sure my stick was on me, and then I jogged around to the sidewalk Bishop was standing on.

"Ay, don't do no stupid shit in here. Let me do all da mutha-fuckin' talkin'," he had the nerve to say once I got next to him. He should've been the last one talking about doing stupid shit when he was the one who killed Leto and triggered everything to begin with. Plus, what the hell he thought I was going here to do? That fool inside had my son's life taken, and the person he was trying to kill was standing right next to me. It was up between us. Bishop must've forgotten who the fuck I was. The whole thing said it was a death trap, but for my revenge, I was willing to take that chance.

"What can I get you guys today?" a woman behind the counter asked when we walked in. "We have the best Spanish lattes around. Or do you prefer a *dark* coffee?" She flirted with Bishop, looking him up and down.

"We ain't come here for no gah damn coffee! Where the owner?" I quizzed.

"What the fuck did I say?" Bishop asked, turning to look at me. I didn't give a damn what the nigga told me to do before we got inside. I was my own man, and I was on my own mission.

"Oh! Just a second," she said and then disappeared around the corner.

"I'on trust this shit." I shook my head, and Bishop ignored me. Munchie begged me not to go, but I told her I had to. I was the one who suggested she link with Baby Jo so she wouldn't be alone.

"This way," the cashier said when she reappeared about a minute later, and we followed her around the corner. She led us to a door and then walked away without saying anything.

"What the fuck?" I asked, watching her until I didn't see her anymore. Then the door came open, and a guy dressed in black waved us inside. We stepped through the door, and it slammed shut behind us.

"Arms up," he instructed, and I looked like I smelled shit.

"We just tryna talk. You ain't 'bout to search me," I informed him.

"Then leave," he simply said.

"It's cool." Bishop stepped forward and raised his arms up to get searched, and I looked at the nigga like he had two heads. *What the fuck was he on?* The guy searched him, and when he got to Bishop's gun, he took it off him.

"You can get this back when you leave. Do you plan on joining the meeting, or will you be waiting in the car?" he asked, looking at me.

"Man, here," I said, passing him my gun. I'd be damned if Bishop's crazy ass was going in without me. That nigga would make a deal with the devil if it suited him. I couldn't trust no shit like that.

"Down the hall." He pointed after taking the gun from me.

"Let's go," Bishop said, and then we walked off. "Don't fuck this up," he said once we got to the door at the end of the hall.

"Don't you fuck this up," I shot back, and he knocked on the door.

"Enter!" a voice yelled out, and Bishop twisted the doorknob and pushed it open. When we walked inside, we saw a black man sitting behind the desk, and that stopped me dead in my tracks. Everyone who worked there looked Hispanic. His right-hand man we met up with was Hispanic, and so was Leto. So I wasn't expecting to see no nigga running the Cocaine Cartel. That shit threw me for a loop, and Bishop hit my arm to make me snap out of it. All I wanted to know was who the fuck that nigga was. "The two of you can have a seat," he said, pointing at the two chairs in front of the desk.

"I'm good. I'll stand." I shrugged.

"You'll sit!" he yelled, standing up, and I cocked my head to the side.

"Boy, who da fuck you talkin' to? We both know this ain't no friendly meeting, so stop the bullshit and cut to the chase. The fuck a nigga doin' running the Cocaine Cartel anyway?" I questioned, and he started to laugh.

"I like you." He nodded his head.

"I ain't wit' the gay shit." I threw my hand up.

"Man, sit da fuck down and shut da hell up," Bishop demanded through clenched teeth.

"Funny. Take a seat. I have some things I want to talk to the two of you about."

"I bet you do," I mumbled, and we went to take a seat. The guy at the door had fucked up by not searching me because I still had another gun on me. And I was waiting on the perfect time to use it. I'd shoot my way out that bitch if I had to.

"I'll answer your first question," the plug said, looking at me, and I looked at him like I was confused. "You wanted to know what a *nigga* was doing running the Cocaine Cartel. So here's your answer. A lot of people don't know that I'm the one running this shit, and there's a reason why. I married the wife of a cartel boss a few months after he was murdered. Was we fucking around before he got killed? Yes, we was but only because he violated her in a lot of ways we won't discuss. After his death, she married me, and I took over because this cartel originated from her family. But we didn't want everyone knowing that I was leader, because they wouldn't have taken orders from me. Some of them actually formed a strong bond with her husband, and if they knew she allowed someone else to come in to take over instead of passing it on to another family member, they would've been pissed. So now, the majority of the cartel think it's being ran by her younger brother, Jesus, but that's not true. Jesus is actually my right-hand man, who you two have already met. He has a family and business of his own. Therefore, he didn't want the responsibility of being the boss. But his sister was able to talk him into at least pretending like he was the boss. To the family, he's in charge, and to customers, he's the right-hand man because everyone knows the actual boss would never get his hands dirty, which brings me to the reason why I've told you all of this and called for a meeting today."

"Which is?" I asked after he'd paused for a second too long.

"Leto is her son, and he was killed in Florida. So I stopped supplying anyone in Florida until I got to the bottom of this shit," he said, and I saw Bishop clench his jaw. "You see, Leto found out the truth about me being the one in charge. He didn't like that, so he killed his own mother and fled. After that, we put a price tag on his head, but no one could find him. Then we resulted in putting out a rumor that he was getting high off the product and got disowned just to see how people would start moving when they found that out. You two took the bait after that information was released and started snooping around to find me. That told us that one of you was the one who killed him."

"So you killed m—" I started to say *my son* but quickly stopped myself. "His son."

"Come again?" His eyebrow cocked.

"You sent someone to shoot up Bishop's car and killed his fucking son instead! Nigga, fuck whatever else you got to say!" I jumped up and pulled my gun out.

"Wait a minute," he said, staying calmy. "For one, you don't want to do that. You'll never make it out of here alive. There's more people around than you think that are paid to protect me. And you see that door?" he quizzed, pointing behind him. "You don't want it to open, because if it does, your head and body will be leaving here separately. And you pulling a fucking gun out is all the reason I need to kill your ass. Sit the fuck down," he ordered.

"You heard him," Bishop cut his eyes at me and made me want to jaw him. But I wasn't backing down until I found the underlying cause of shit. He might've not gave a damn about BJ, but I did, and I was going to ride for my family that he thought was his.

"Nah! BJ is dead behind this shit!"

"Listen," the plug said, standing up, "I wasn't after revenge when I wanted to know who killed Leto. They did this family a favor by finding and killing him, and I'm a man of my word. There was a million-dollar tag on his head for whoever killed him, and that's what I called you here for... to pay you and triple your supply with no extra charge. I'm grateful for your help. I didn't call you here to kill you, because if I wanted you dead, I wouldn't be sitting here telling you my history. Think about it for a second, and if I sent someone to shoot up a car, everybody in that bitch would've been dead," he said, and it actually started to make sense. "I'm not a sloppy type of man. I do everything nice and neat. Besides, if that was the case, I would've just called a meeting and killed you then instead. We do business together, so it's not like I couldn't have arranged it. You two do great business and bring in a lot of money, and that's the only reason why I'm explaining this shit to you because obviously, you are hurt, and you have the right to be," the plug explained further, and I looked over at Bishop who had a strange look on his face.

"So if you didn't do it, who the fuck did?"

"I'm not sure, but take this," he said and got up from his seat before pulling a suitcase around the desk. "It's the money for killing Leto. Did you two have beef with someone out in the streets?"

"I don't fucking know. Shit, I thought we was beefing with you," I said honestly, and he chuckled.

"I beef with no one, but let me know if there's anything else I can do to help. If not, you're dismissed," he said and then turned his back to us to go look out the window.

"Let's go," Bishop said, finally standing up, and I followed him out the office after grabbing the big ass suitcase.

"You believe him?" I asked once Bishop and I made it back to the car and got inside.

"I do," was all he said as I started up the car and pulled off. How the fuck could he be so sure?

Something just didn't feel right, and maybe Bishop knew they weren't the ones who killed BJ all along, and that was why he wasn't after them. But if that was the truth, why would he lie? Better yet, why would he even bring me on this trip if he knew the truth would come out? Not unless that was his plan all along, and he was trying to cover his own tracks for some reason. *Was he the one who killed my son?*

21

MUNCHIE

FIVE MONTHS LATER

I sat on the couch with my feet tucked under me as I fed my baby girl. I'd given birth to her two months and named her Princess because that was exactly what she was. And I didn't want her to ever forget that. I looked into her grayish puppy dog eyes, and she'd definitely got that from Bishop, but they were shaped like mine. She was the perfect mix of both of us with milk-chocolate skin, and a head full of thick, curly hair.

She was a chunky baby like BJ had been, and I took a deep breath at the thought of him. He stayed on my mind daily, and if it wasn't for me having Princess, I would've given up on life as soon as I found out my son was dead. Most of the time, I didn't feel like I could get through the day, but I would always touch my stomach to give me a reason to push on, and now that she was finally here, all I had to do was look at her face. It was always comforting, but the depression was still there, and staying in the house didn't do anything to help, but I was making it. Baby Jo was still coming to Florida often and getting me out of the house to do things for the wedding.

She never wanted to bother me with the wedding, but I'd told her repeatedly I needed something else to focus on, so it was helping more than she knew. Stunna and his mother were staying in contact with me as well. Mary always wanted to sit on the phone and pray over me while Stunna had me buying stuff for Jody behind her back. Since their wedding was on Christmas Day, they would be spending that entire week in Florida, and I couldn't wait. Raheem did what he could to help too, but being that I was still staying with Bishop, it was only so much he could do.

Bishop, on the other hand, wasn't much help at all, not that I ever expected differently. He was always at that casino, and since they'd made it twenty-four hours, he had put a big ass couch in there that had a pullout bed. It was already a full bathroom with a shower inside the office, so he was damn near living there. I wouldn't have cared if we didn't have a newborn baby that I needed help with. I was going through just as much as him, but that didn't mean I got to clock the fuck out and decide when I was and wasn't going to do for our baby. My job as a full-time mother didn't stop, so his job as a father shouldn't have either, and it pissed me the hell off with him even more.

"Mrs. King, I'm all done in the kitchen. Is it sum else you need fo' me to do?" Ciara walked into the living room and asked as I placed my baby's bottle down on the couch next to me and placed her on my shoulder to burp her.

"What I tell you about calling me that?" I smiled.

"Oh, my B, Munchie," she corrected herself, but I knew she would forget again the next time because that was what she'd been told to call me.

Ciara was eighteen, and she'd just graduated high school in June. She was a sweet girl that went to church with Jody's mama, and that was who recommended her since she didn't have plans of attending college. She had three younger siblings that she basically helped her mother raise since they were born. After meeting with her, I knew she would be perfect for the position. Since my mental wasn't all the way there on most days, I didn't hesitate to find the help I needed, and Ciara was perfect. She babysat whenever I needed her to.

She also came over a few days out the week to clean the house, and I only added that to the job as a way for her to make more money. I knew what it was like to be that age and dead ass broke, but at least she graduated high school, even if her home-life wasn't the best. Her mother had stopped going to church a long time ago, but Ciara still went and took her siblings with her faithfully. She was a bright girl, but she'd told me school wasn't for her since she barely graduated high school. I still tried to talk her into signing up for classes in the spring though since it was September and fall classes at the community college had already started.

"You good, girl. You be making me feel old. I'm only about to be twenty-five at the end of the year." I laughed.

"I know, but Mrs. Jackson would kill me if she knew I was up in here calling you by your first name. She told me it was a respect thing since I was working for you," she explained right as Princess burped.

"And I'm telling you, Munchie is just fine. I don't like that damn last name," I fussed, and she started laughing.

"You funny."

"But if you're done in the kitchen, that's all I need for the day. Let me get you an Uber, and I'll Cash App you for today's work."

"Okay," she said, excitedly and took a seat on the couch.

I was paying her a thousand dollars every time she came. That was probably more than the job was worth, but this was a big ass mansion, and I wanted to help her out any way I could since she'd been talking about wanting to get a car. Sometimes the only thing a person needed was someone who was willing to help and invest in them. That always made the difference, and I wished I had someone who'd done the same for me. Instead, I ended up leaning on a man for support, and my life was turned upside down. I didn't even blame Bishop anymore, because I'd played my part in shit as well, and at that point, I was just going with the flow for the sake of peace.

"Alright. Can you change her for me while I go upstairs to get my phone," I said, standing up with Princess still in my arms.

"Of course," Ciara said, holding her hands out for the baby.

I walked over and passed Princess to her, and then I grabbed the wipes and a diaper and placed them on the couch next to her. Once she laid Princess down, I left out and went upstairs. Ciara had been coming over since a couple of weeks after Princess was born. So she'd been with us for almost two months and I felt comfortable with her. It didn't hurt that someone I already knew recommended her because I wasn't about to just trust anyone with my baby. People were crazy as hell, and I never knew what a person was truly capable of.

When I walked into my bedroom, I grabbed my phone off the nightstand and pulled up the Uber app. After it said one was on the way and would be there in about thirty minutes, I went to Cash App and sent her money. Then I headed back downstairs, and when I walked into the living room, I saw Raheem standing in the middle of the floor. I hadn't even heard him knock or ring the doorbell.

"Oh, hey. I didn't know you was here."

"Yeah, Ciara let me in," he said, looking around.

"Where's Bishop?" I asked, even though I already knew. It was only going on five, so it wouldn't see him no time soon, if at all.

"He still at the casino. I had to make some... um... runs," Rah said, looking over at Ciara.

"Oh okay." I went back to sit on the couch as Ciara rocked Princess in her arms.

"I needed to talk to you."

"Okay, hold on," I said as my phone started ringing, and I saw it was Baby Jo calling.

"A'ight." Raheem walked out of the living room, and I figured he went in the kitchen or something.

"Hello?" I answered.

"Hey, boo. Um, you busy?"

"No, not really. What's up?"

"Oh, yo' friend Dula ain't there?" she asked, sounding annoyed when she said Dula's name.

"Girl, no. I told you I haven't heard much from Dula or really seen her like that since everything happened with BJ," I sighed.

"Fake ass hoe. I didn't like that girl no way. And what type of friend just falls back after some shit like that?" Baby Jo asked, and I knew she was ready to go off all over again. When I first told her that, she went in on Dula.

"You know she can't have kids, Jody. It might've been depressing for her or something. I don't know."

"That's bullshit! But whatever. I'm not gon' keep getting on to you 'bout that damn girl, but if I was you I would cut her ass completely," she said, and I just knew her eyes were rolling.

"What's up?" I asked, trying to get to the purpose of the phone call.

"I'm pregnant."

"Whaaaaaat!" I yelled. "Oh my goodness! Congratulations! I'm so happy for you and Stunna. That's great," I gushed.

"Yeeaaaah…"

"Wait, what's wrong?" I quizzed because all the energy she had before seemed to be gone when she said that.

"He doesn't know yet, and I'm scared to tell him," she sighed.

"Why?"

"Because, Munch, I don't know if it's the time for a baby. We haven't even discussed having a child together. I don't want anything to change between us."

"Why would anything change? I'm sure he'll be over the moon when he finds out. That nigga love the hell out of you, and everyone knows it. A baby shouldn't change anything, and y'all are already raising your girls together and getting married. Trust me, you worrying for nothing because you know that man don't play 'bout you," I said. She had to be crazy if she doubted Stunna in any type of way because that man made it clear he wasn't going to play with her from the jump.

"You might be right. Girl, I pissed on that stick and started freaking the fuck out. It reminded me of when I discovered I was pregnant with Sunny."

"Well, I'm telling you now, don't get to popping no damn pills, or I'ma come to Nevada and kick your ass my-damn-self," I said, and she busted out laughing.

"Biiiiitch, don't fucking do me! Ain't it funny how far we've come?"

"Yeah, it's really crazy."

"But I'll be back next week. I'm going to keep having to get this damn dress altered. I should've known something was up when I started gaining weight out the blue."

"Okay, and you still look good, so don't even trip."

"Did you ever go and pick out your dress, or you haven't had time?"

"Haven't had time, but we can find me one when you come back. I know the wedding is only a few months away now. I just wanted to wait until after I gave birth and returned to my normal size, but it don't look like that's happening. You gaining weight, and I'm losing it." I laughed a little.

"Because you still don't eat like you need to be," she fussed, and I sucked my teeth.

"My appetite just isn't there."

"Tell Rah to get you some weed," she said, and I didn't know why I hadn't thought about that sooner. I desperately needed something to keep me at bay. I hadn't smoked since before I found out I was pregnant with BJ.

"I might do that shit for real."

"Okay. Well, Stunna and the girls pulling back up now."

"Alright, let me know how it goes."

"K, bye."

"Bye," I said and hung up. I looked at my phone and saw the Uber was pulling through the gates. "She went to sleep that fast?" I asked, looking at Ciara, and she nodded. I got up and grabbed Princess, so I could swaddle her in her blanket and put her in the bassinet next to the couch.

"She milk wasted," Ciara joked, and I laughed.

"Girl, she must be. The Uber just pulled up though. Did you get the money on your Cash App?" I asked and she looked at her phone as she got up.

"Yeah, thanks, Miss Munchie. I'll see y'all in a couple days," she said as she went to grab her bag that was sitting in a chair.

"Okay, love."

"Bye, Rah!" she yelled out.

"A'ight, Ciara!" he hollered from the kitchen as I walked her to the front door. I watched her walk outside and jump in the Uber before closing the door. Then I went back to the living room.

"When you get this?" Raheem walked in the living room and questioned after I'd placed Princess in her bassinet. He was holding my Cartier LOVE bracelet that I'd left on the counter in the kitchen.

"It was an anniversary gift from Bishop."

"Then why it got BJ's name on the inside wit' the words *my angel*? He wasn't gone yet when you got this, right?"

"Right," I said, thinking about that for the first time because it hadn't hit me until that moment.

"I think I know why Bishop walked away from that drive-by without a fucking scratch," he said, and my heart started to pound in my chest.

22

BABY JO
LATER THAT NIGHT

"That food was hittin' like a muthafucka! Gah damn, you know how to whip that shit *up*," Stunna said, sliding into the bed next to me, and I laughed.

"Well, you know how I do. Know I don't play games. Best cook around," I bragged, turning on my side to face him as he lay on his back.

"Don't let Moms here you say that shit. She be ready to go to war 'bout her food." He laughed.

"Who food better?" I asked, tilting my head back and poking my lips out.

"My baby's food better." He lifted his head up and pecked my lips.

"Yeah, that's what I thought," I joked. "How was the baking class with the girls earlier?"

"You saw what we looked like when we got back. It was a damn mess. They was in there throwing flour and everything. Had to break them folks off a couple racks. Ajay broke the damn stove door by trying to hang on it. The shit wasn't on at the time, but I couldn't get her, because I was chasing Sunny around the room."

"Aww, my poor baby. I'm sorry I couldn't make it," I smiled at him and reached to stroke his thick beard.

"We still rocked that shit out and baked our cookies before we punished them hoes. They was hitting too. We didn't make it to the cake, but as long as they had fun and shit, I was happy and still enjoyed myself. You know me and my girls like to eat. But I'm glad your headache went away. And you still cooked dinner too? They don't make 'em like you no more," he bragged.

"What they make 'em like, Stunna?" I raised an eyebrow.

"Don't start." He laughed, and I joined in. "But nah, you straight for real? That headache hit you out of nowhere."

I got silent after that. When I got off the phone with Munchie earlier, I greeted them at the door and took the girls upstairs to get them cleaned up for dinner. When I came back down, we all sat at the table and enjoyed a new recipe I tried out. The girls were hyper as fuck because they ate all of them cookies from the baking class. If I was there, we would've made them, ate one, and wrapped the rest up for later so their dinner wouldn't be ruined. Of course Stunna didn't enforce that rule and let them go a fool eating them cookies because he was stuffing his face too. Then he was looking crazy when they didn't want to finish their dinner. I wasn't going to force them to eat if they weren't hungry, and I guess we didn't think things through when we planned to take them to class. Anyway, after we finished up dinner, we watched a movie, and then I went and helped the girls get ready for bed since they took their baths as soon as they got back. Once they were in their rooms and fast asleep, Stunna and I took a shower together. So I hadn't really had the time to tell him the news. Munchie was right when she said he would probably be happy, but I was still scared. Shit had been so rough for me during my first pregnancy, and I didn't want to fuck up. I didn't want the baby to change things for the worse because I' saw that shit happen to many times before, and I didn't want that for us. I wanted to be on the exact same page about everything.

"There's actually something I need to tell you," I finally said.

"What is it?" he asked, placing his hand on my bare thigh that was exposed.

"I don't know how to say it."

"Spit it out. Not unless you 'bout to tell me you don't wanna marry a nigga. Then you can swallow that shit," he said, and I busted out laughing and slapped his arm.

"Oh my God. I'm so fucking sick of you."

"I ain't playing." He looked at me, but I couldn't stop laughing.

"Stop. You know I would never say no shit like that. I'm pregnant," I said, and the fact that he had me hollering in that bed made it a little easier. Where in the hell did he come up with the crazy shit he said? It never got old to me, and I loved that about him.

"Say that again."

"I'm pregnant, babe."

"Stop playing."

"Marlon, I'm not playing." I used his real name so he could know just how serious I was, but I wasn't expecting for the nut to hop out of bed and start crip walking across the damn carpet.

"If you don't sit the fuck down!" I yelled at him, laughing.

"Ohhhh... yeeaaaah." He pulled his shirt over his head and started flexing his muscles.

"Byeeee!" I hollered, cracking up. He was too much. "Stunna, stop!" I screeched as he grabbed my ankles and pulled me to the edge of the bed.

"You having my baby?" he asked, laying on me until our faces were only inches apart.

"Yes." I smiled right before he kissed me, and I didn't know why I expected anything different from him. I guess it was still certain things I was insecure about, but he always managed to make me feel better.

"I know. I ain't been shooting the club up every night for

nothing. You think it's too late to give our baby a twin?" he asked.

"Oh my God! You so dumb." I covered my face, and he moved my hands and stuck his thick tongue in my mouth.

"Mmm, I want that pussy and ass in my face," he said after pulling back, and I knew what that meant. He stood up and got naked, and I did the same before laying on the bed with my head hanging off the side.

Stunna walked over to where I was and then leaned down and wrapped his arms around my waist before lifting me off the bed. When he stood up straight, I was upside down, and his dick was in my face. I wrapped my arms around his waist and started sucking on his dick when I felt his tongue lick my pussy. I wasn't even scared that he would drop me, because it wasn't our first time doing sixty-nine standing up. When it came to sex, that was the type of shit he had me doing.

We made love in the bed, but when we fucked, we did it anywhere—standing up, on chairs, on the floor, in the kitchen, on the balconies, on the front porch. It really didn't matter to us as long as the kids were gone. There was difference between us making love and us fucking was when we fucked, we went all out. Stunna was hung like a horse, and that dick damn near killed me the first time I had it. It was so long and girthy I didn't know what to do with it, but I learned quickly.

"Mmm," I moaned as Stunna dipped his tongue inside of me.

I almost lost focus for a second, but I got back to what I was doing and started eating his dick up. I was moving my neck like a rooster as I went crazy. And the wilder I got, the more intense Stunna got with licking and slurping on my pussy. I knew it was probably going to be a while before we could do the position again, so I didn't hold back. It wasn't long before my legs started to shake and Stunna nutted down my throat while I squirted in his face.

"Shit!" he yelled after laying me on the bed.

"You know I love that shit," I said in a seductive voice as I moved to lay on my pillow.

"Fuck nah. Where you goin'? You know better. Bring that ass here," he demanded.

"Bae, I can't even get up," I whined.

"Come on," he said, reaching out for my hand, and I grabbed it. He helped me get right back out the bed and then slapped my ass cheek. "Sexy self. Don't play wit' me," he whispered in my ear before leaning down and picking me up.

I wrapped my legs around him, and he lifted me up a little before bringing me back down on his hard dick. I wrapped my arms around his neck and held on to it like I was on the monkey bars while he adjusted his hands to grip my thighs. Then he started bouncing me up and down and fucked me standing up. My head was tilted back, and I enjoyed every inch of himself he shoved inside of me. My toes were curled up, and I bit down on my bottom lip.

"Mmm."

"I'm so fucking deep in this pussy. Tell me to go deeper."

"Go deeper. Ah!" I yelled out when he slammed me down on his dick.

"Ooo shit, I love you fucking much."

"I love you too."

"You fuckin' better," he said, making me even wetter. Five minutes later, he was nutting all in me before we moved to the bed for another round, and that was exactly how my ass had gotten pregnant to begin with.

✻ 23 ✻

BISHOP

I pulled out the casino parking lot and headed in the direction of my estate. It was going on three in the morning, and lately the casino was where I'd been spending the majority of my time. I had to stay busy, or I didn't know what the fuck I would do. Shit with the cartel had been crazy, and it'd been on my mind since Raheem and I left California. I just knew they were the ones who'd pulled that shit and shot my car the fuck up.

As soon as I pulled away from Baby Jo's mama's house, someone got behind me and followed me all the way down the street. When I got to the stop sign and stopped, I saw them pulling around me instead of behind me. That was when I tried to step on the gas and grabbed my gun at the same time because I didn't know what the hell they was on. As expected, they started shooting, and I returned the shots. I wasn't watching where I was going and ended up slamming into a car that was parked on the side of the street.

The other car continued to bust at my ass after I wrecked and my damn gun jammed. That was when I thought to get in the back seat to cover BJ, but the car was pulling off by then, and when I turned around, I saw BJ had been riddled with bullets in his car seat. I called the police and tried to call Munchie, but she didn't answer, and my phone eventually went dead. After the cops and shit came, I was questioned and taken to the hospital while BJ was carried off the scene in a body bag. I spent that entire night in the hospital, and I was discharged the first thing the next morning once they was sure I was straight.

Everything after that had been hell. Munchie didn't respect my decision to have BJ cremated, but I couldn't sit through another fucking funeral and watch another child be buried. I just wasn't about to do it, and she wasn't going to force me to do it. I knew I was wrong for not getting her consent beforehand, but I also knew she would've never agreed to that shit. Everything wasn't always about her or how she felt, but of course she thought differently. Things seemed to be really getting on the right track for us before all that happened.

We were back at peace around one another and communicating well while respecting boundaries and all that bullshit. I'd been hopeful that things were returning to the way they were before she got locked up, but that was all it was... wishful thinking. I shook my head as I made a turn at the light and rode in complete silence. I was only going home because I wanted to rest in a real damn bed for the night. I couldn't stand being at my place anymore, and Munchie was the reason for that.

She blamed me for everything that happened, and I could see it all in her eyes whenever she looked at me. She even asked why I let that shit happen like I didn't do everything in my power that I could that night. So to avoid feeling guilty about some shit that wasn't my fault, I stayed away as much as possible.

Work kept me busy anyway. After that trip to California, the plug stayed true to his word and tripled our supply free of charge. That shit, along with the casino, had me rolling in more money than ever. Since I was always at the casino, I wanted to start pushing drugs out of that bitch, but I promised Stunna I would keep that shit away from business. And since he'd did so much, I respected that promise and kept my word.

Anyway, when I found out the cartel really wasn't the ones responsible for BJ's death, I didn't know what to do. But I did know they were telling the truth. Raheem was acting like a fucking idiot, and I didn't like the way he handled things. Dumbass nigga could've got us both killed. I'd been telling him to chill with that shit for months, and for some reason he felt some type of way.

BJ was my son, and if I said we needed to hold off on shit, that was just what it was. I'd lost my fucking son, and I wasn't in the mood to jump right out and get with the dumb shit. I needed to get my head on right and my facts straights, but he had me wishing I never told him it was the cartel to begin with because at the time, I really didn't know. I'd gone on a killing spree after Bella died, and it was multiple people who could've felt some type of way about me. It just made more sense for it be the cartel with everything going on. I never told Raheem about the problem with them, because the nigga got ignorant at times.

I didn't want him fucking up shit before I could figure out, because originally, I'd planned to tell him. I just changed my mind, and maybe that was a mistake on my end, but after the way Rah acted in Cali I was clearly right. The whole purpose of the trip for me was to see what they were on because the plug wasn't calling the meeting for no reason, but I couldn't tell Raheem shit. Going to California was risky from the jump when I thought they wanted me dead, but at that point, I'd lost so much I really didn't care if I made it back to Florida or not.

Anyway, ever since then, Raheem seemed to have an unspoken problem with me, and I guess it was because of the way I handled things on that trip. I didn't give a fuck though, because I was the boss for a reason, not his ass. So he could keep leaving work early every day and making runs without me for now. It didn't fucking matter, and he was dumber than I thought if he believed I wasn't trying to get revenge for my son, but fuck that nigga. I hadn't been feeling the way he was moving in a long time ,and when the time was right, I would be cutting his ass off.

Shit just wasn't right with him, so he had to go. In the meantime, I had to focus on making shit right between Munchie and me again. It didn't matter if she made me not want to be around her or not; I still loved her.

We'd lost too much not to be there for each other and our daughter. That was what it all boiled down to. Even if I hadn't been the best father, but that wasn't my first fuckup, and it sure as hell wouldn't be my last. I just needed Munchie to start back riding for me like she did in the beginning. And maybe it was fucked up of me to expect her to do that after everything I'd done to us, but I did. She was my wife, and it was until death did we part. I meant that shit with everything in me.

After I finally made it home an hour later, I parked and turned my car off. I'd been driving slow just so I could have some time to myself to actually hear myself think for once. I pulled my phone, that had been vibrating the whole time I drove home, out my pocket. When I looked at the screen, I saw it had been Brandy calling me back-to-back. The phone started to ring again, and her name appeared on the screen, but I didn't answer it.

I didn't have shit to say to Brandy. She hadn't been around for neither of my kids' deaths, and I knew I never told her about having Bella, but how the fuck could I? We didn't talk like that, and when I did call her phone and tell her everything, the first thing she asked was why didn't I tell her about Bella sooner. That was a mile away from the point when my daughter died. And that shit pissed me off, so I hung up on her. I thought she would at least check back in, but nope.

Then when BJ died, she told me she was sorry to hear that and maybe it was for the best. That told me everything I needed to know about her. So I hadn't hit her up since. My phone finally stopped ringing, and then a text came through from her that said she needed to talk to me. I didn't have time for that shit. Therefore, I blocked her number. If she was calling me, it meant something was wrong. That was the only time I ever heard from or saw her, when she needed something, but when she was up and life was great, it was fucking crickets. Sister or not, fuck her.

I finally got out of the car and made my way inside. When I walked into the living room, a lamp came on, and Munchie was sitting in the corner with one leg across the other one like Taraji P. Henson off that damn *Acrimony* movie. Instead of smoking a cigarette though, she was smoking a blunt, and I frowned and looked around. What in the hell did she have going on? It was too late for her shit.

"What's good?" I questioned. "And why da fuck you in here smoking a blunt? No, when the fuck did you start smoking weed at all? And where da hell my daughter?" I interrogated.

"Why did you get me this?" she asked, then tossed something at my feet. I looked at her like she was crazy as I leaned down. When I picked up what she tossed, I saw it was her Cartier LOVE bracelet.

"What you mean why I got you this? It was a fucking anniversary present. Man, don't start wit' that retarded ass shit. For real, I ain't in the mood, Munchie. I'm not even playing right now," I said because what the hell was the problem now? Damn.

"I don't giva fuck what you in the mood for!" she yelled, jumping up, and I started shaking my head.

"Munchie, you know I'm not da type to beat yo' ass, but on God, if you run up I'ma lay yo' crazy ass out here in here. I said I'm not in da fucking mood!"

"So do something!" she hollered, running up any-damn-way and trying to swing on me.

"Bruh, move. Gone 'head," I said, pushing her ass back with my arm. She had gotten a little too comfortable with putting her damn hands on me when she got mad.

"Or what! Or what!"

"What da fuck is wrong witchu!" I yelled in her face after grabbing both of her hands. "And to think, I came to make shit right wit' you, but this exactly why I stay gone now. You either doing too much or not enough."

"Why did you put the words *My Angel* on that bracelet, Bishop? You gave me that shit, and my son died the exact same night."

"Ay, ay, what you tryin' to get at?" My face twisted up because I just knew she wasn't implying what I thought she was.

"You killed my son?"

"Is you fucking serious!" I yelled and let her hands go.

"Answer the question." She crossed her arms over her chest.

"I would never do no shit like that, and you sick as hell for even thinking that I would. I put that shit on the bracelet because I heard you callin' him that more than once. What the fuck is wrong witchu, bruh? Better yet, why every time you talk about BJ, you saying *my son*? Huh!" I asked, ready to flip out on her like never before. "Oh, you quiet now. You better open yo' gah damn mouth up and speak. Don't play wit' me," I barked.

"Bishop," she said softly, and I shook my head.

"Nah, you on sum other shit. For real." I shook my head at her again.

"I'm sorry. I don't know. I seen the bracelet, and the words just stood out to me. I let my thoughts get the best of me, and I keep saying my son because you wasn't there for him like you was with Bella. You ran over there almost every damn day, but when I moved out, it was fuck me and him," she reasoned, and my face relaxed a little.

"You never should've left, Munchie. And I found out about you wiring money from my account too. I know that's how you paid for that damn house. If you wanted it that bad, all you had to do was ask."

"You wouldn't have bought it," she finally said after looking shocked that I knew about that.

"You damn right. We belong together, and I'm sorry I snapped on you like that, but don't ever accuse me of no shit like that. That's fucked up, and a nigga already fucked up enough. I don't need you puttin' no shit like that on me. I apologize for cremating BJ, and I should've apologized sooner, but I just couldn't another funeral. Forgive me," I said, stepping closer to her and placing my hand on her waist.

"Bishop."

"Munchie, please. We both have said some fucked-up shit tonight and made accusations. Let's just squash this shit. Matter fact, our five-year anniversary is coming up soon. Let's have a party and start fresh. We've never actually celebrated our anniversary before. It was always something going on. Let's do it right this next time around."

"Bishop," she said again, but I wasn't trying to hear what she had to say. I needed to know everything was going to be alright because she knew I couldn't let her go. It wasn't in me.

"Please, baby. One last chance to fix this shit between us, and if you still want to leave after that, I'll let you. I put it on the kids, baby. It won't be easy, but I'll do that for you. I promise," I said, and she sighed.

"Okay, Bishop," she eventually agreed, and I hugged her with a blank expression on my face, feeling like she was doing the same.

24

MUNCHIE
A FEW MONTHS LATER

"Mommy Jo, can I eat it?" Ajay asked Jody as she pointed at the gingerbread houses we were making. I decided the name Baby Jo wasn't fitting for her anymore because she'd outgrown the name. She'd overcome so much and transformed into an amazing woman. Her strength was undeniable, and Jody seriously deserved the world in my eyes, so it was great to see her finally getting it.

"No, girl. We gotta finish decorating them first." Jody laughed.

It was Christmas Eve, and we were at Bishop's place in the dining room. It was getting late, and we'd celebrated Christmas that morning since the wedding was on Christmas Day. Stunna, Baby Jo, and the girls agreed to come stay with us while they were in town so they didn't have to spend the holidays in a hotel. I knew they didn't mind, but it was a lot more comforting having them over. I had never really been a fan of the holidays, and with BJ gone, it definitely wasn't exciting.

If anything, it was depressing as hell, and I think that was why Jody agreed to come stay with us while they were in town. At least with her over, I had ways to keep my mind off things. It warmed my heart to watch her girls open their presents, and Bishop and I opened the presents we got for Princess, who was five months now. Of course she didn't know what was going on, but it still made me happy. Jody and I woke up early to make a big breakfast with the help of Ajay and Sunny, who'd been bouncing off the walls since.

After breakfast, we opened gifts, and it was going on noon once we finished. Then the guys kicked back to watch TV and drink beer while Jody and I got ourselves and the kids ready to go. We didn't want them to have to sit in the house all day long, although I doubted they would've minded with all the new toys they got. Plus, Jody and Stunna hadn't even brought all their gifts along on the trip. They had plenty of time to play with that stuff though, so we took them to a place that had an ice rink inside. Ajay and Sunny seemed to enjoy it, and even Jody wasn't that bad at it, but I could hardly stay on my damn feet. Princess had been left at home with Stunna, Bishop, and Raheem, and it felt good to finally have some help with her.

Bishop seemed like he was really trying to work on our relationship over the last few months, but it honestly wasn't anything to work on. I only agreed to the anniversary party because he caught me up constantly saying that BJ was my son, and that was my mistake. So I had to play things differently after that. Raheem was the one who put it in my head that Bishop killed BJ, and I was livid by the time he made it home. Raheem was angry too, but I told him I would handle it, and I felt I did just that.

Bishop's reason for putting that on the bracelet was accurate, because I really did call BJ that from time to time. I just didn't think about it when I had Raheem in my face going the fuck off about what he was going to do to Bishop. When I told him Bishop's excuse, he wasn't buying it at all, but it was enough to make him chill the hell out because he was ready to kill Bishop. Now that all of that had died down, I had to worry about the fucking anniversary party. Raheem was pissed when he found out I agreed to it because he said that wasn't part of the plan.

I didn't know what the hell else he expected me to do after he had me looking like a fool and accusing Bishop of killing *his own son*. So he was mad at me, but it was his fault I ended up back at that damn estate anyway. The sooner he got me out of the shit like he promised, the better, but he wanted to have an attitude that he'd kept up for the last few months. I didn't have time for that shit, so we'd kind of been going back and forth about the situation. If it wasn't for the fact I had Princess and thought us leaving would set Bishop off, I definitely wouldn't have still been at that mansion.

"I can't believe the guys decided to go to the casino for Stunna's bachelor party," Jody said, rolling her eyes. We'd made it back home from skating a while ago and was working on gingerbread houses.

"Right. I thought we agreed that everyone was going to stay in and work on this gingerbread village." I laughed, looking over in the swing next to me and rocking Princess. She was still asleep, and I wasn't surprised because noise didn't bother her at all.

"We should've known that was a lie."

"I blame Bishop. He was so anxious to go somewhere and do something."

"Stunna got a mind of his own, but if it was really a problem, believe me, he wouldn't have been going anywhere. I wanted him to enjoy his night though, so that was why I didn't say anything. I just knew I wasn't going to be doing a bachelorette party."

"I hope it wasn't because you was worried about me. I told you've multiple times that you didn't have to dim you happiness or wedding for me. I want you to enjoy everything to the fullest."

"Well, I'ma worry 'bout you regardless."

"I'm fine, Jo. I promise."

"I know you're not, and I don't expect you to be so soon. It's just now about to be a year since everything happened, so don't feel the need to rush the healing process. Ut takes time," she looked across the table at me, and I looked down.

"Yeah... I know. Some days are better than others, but I'm getting through it."

"Just know I appreciate you still being here for my big day and helping out with everything. It really means a lot."

"Aww," I said, placing my hands on my chest.

"Shut up, Munchie Wunchie." She tossed something at me, making me laugh. "So how you feel about this anniversary party coming up in two weeks?" she questioned, and I looked at the ceiling.

"Girl!"

"I know, right? I would say I hate I can't make it since we'll still be on our honeymoon. But baby, I'm not tryin' to be at that fake ass shit. I'm just being real." She laughed.

"I don't want to be there myself. I hate I didn't take your advice that night at BJ's baby shower and come clean. Now I have Princess, and that's made shit so much more complicated," I sighed, knowing I didn't have anyone to blame but myself for that, but I didn't regret my daughter.

"Boo, I love you, but I gave you all the advice I could on that shit. It's beyond me." She shook her head.

"You right. I'll figure it out one way or another." I picked up a pack of icing and opened it to squirt on my gingerbread house. Jody was doing the same while Ajay started eating the gum drops, and Sunny was sucking on a pack of icing. I smiled at them. They were the cutest.

"Before it's too late, I hope."

"Yessss, Jo, damn," I said, and she started laughing.

"Don't get mad at me. I'm tired of beating that horse. Oh, and guess what!" she yelled, scaring the shit out of me.

"What? Gon' give me a heart attack."

"Hush, crybaby," she joked. "I don't know how in the hell I forgot to tell you this, but I guess because we've been so busy."

"What happened?" I raised my brows and placed the pack of icing down.

"Guess what." She started smiling big.

"What! You scaring me." I shook my head.

"Girl, please. You sleep in the same house as a damn psychopath every night."

"Fuck you." I laughed.

"Nah, but Stunna wants to adopt Sunny, and I want to adopt Ajay after we're married," she hid her mouth from the girls as she said it in a low voice.

"Really?" I asked excitedly.

"Yes. Do you think it's too soon?"

"No. Y'all can do whatever the hell you want. If that's something you've both decided to do and you're both okay with it, I don't see the problem." I shrugged. "I actually love that for y'all."

"Thanks, Munchie. But you know you can give me your honest opinion, right?"

"That is my honest opinion. You've been behind me for years, and I'm behind you on whatever you want to do too. That's y'all's decision to make, so don't even worry about that."

"I am worried about one thing though," she admitted.

"Give it back, Sunny!" Ajay yelled, and Jody and I both looked over at them.

"What's wrong?" Jody questioned.

"She took my candy," Ajay pouted.

"Sunny, give it back," Jody said, and Sunny shook her head.

"But that's mine!" Ajay fussed, and Sunny reached over to hit her.

"No! No! No!"

"Stop!" Ajay hit her back, and the two started swinging on each other. I started laughing as Jody hopped up to separate them. It wasn't funny, but then again, it was because they were so serious and fighting over gumdrops. I guess they'd been around each other so long now that they really were starting to act just like sisters, even though they already called each other that anyway and actually would be after tomorrow.

"That's it. Both of y'all go in the living room and wait for me to come and take y'all upstairs. It's getting late anyway," Jody said, pushing the gingerbread houses back on the table. Ajay stomped out with her arms crossed over her chest, and Sunny took off running. "I don't know what I'ma do with those two. They went from being the best of friends to fighting every day." She shook her head.

"They are getting older," I laughed.

"Lawd, help me." She threw her hands up in the air as she sat back down.

"So what was you worried about? Stunna's baby mama not giving consent?"

"No. She been signed her rights for Ajay over to him."

"What!" I yelled because that was something I didn't know.

"Yup," Jody said, popping her lips as she pushed some hair that was in her face behind her ear. "My problem is T-Bank."

"You didn't put him on the birth certificate, did you?"

"No, but the lawyer said I would still need consent from her father. Even if that meant having to get a DNA test because there's still no proof that he really is her daddy."

"So tell him that nigga dead. RIP to a fuck nigga. Problem gone." I shrugged.

"Bitch, I am not lying 'bout that shit and be somewhere in somebody's fuckin' jail," she said, and I damn near fell out laughing.

"You right. That ain't the move. So get the DNA test and make his ass sign the rights over."

"I can't do that," she said, looking away from me.

"Why not? You don't think he would sign? Pay his broke ass off. He gon' need that money behind bars."

"Nah... That's not gon' work."

"Why you keep saying that? It has to be some—" I started to say before she cut me off.

"He not her daddy!"

"Wait a damn minute," I said, standing up because I wasn't ready for that. "What?" I asked dramatically, trying to make sure I was hearing her right.

"That ain't her damn daddy, Munchie. Um... You remember when you and Bishop always used to be together and would stick me and Raheem together?"

"Oh hell no!" My mouth dropped open.

❧ 25 ❧

BISHOP

"Let me get another round of that," I said to the bartender.

I was sitting at the bar with Stunna and Raheem at the casino. We were drunk as hell, and we'd been here for the last few hours. The night was straight, and I was ready to get out the house. It'd been a good day though, so I couldn't complain. I hadn't had one in a minute.

I was trying my hardest to do right by Munchie so we could fix shit, but that was hard to do. She refused to move back into our bedroom, and I was trying to respect her wishes. But I was tired of that shit and had slipped back into my old ways without her knowing. A nigga had needs, and they were going to get fulfilled with or without her. But that shit was her fight because I was right in her face and ready to do right, but she still wanted to play with a nigga. And then bitches wondered why their niggas stayed cheating.

It was because they got stingy with their pussy and didn't nobody have time for that when pussy was everywhere. It was cool though, because I knew just how to play shit so I wouldn't get caught. When she decided she was ready to give that pussy up again, I'd think about cutting my side hoe off. But as of now, my side hoe wasn't going nowhere. Hell, she was the only one I could depend on these days anyway.

"A'ight, but after this one, I'm calling it a night. Y'all ain't 'bout to fuck my wedding day up because she mad I stayed out all night with you fools," Stunna said with his eyes low.

"Nigga, shut up. Yo' girl run yo' ass anyway." I waved him off. "Weak ass nigga." I looked at him sideways.

"More like smart ass nigga. I actually love my girl." Stunna laughed.

"Preach," Raheem co-signed, and I looked at him funny.

"What y'all tryin' to say?" I scrunched my eyebrows together.

"Man, you know good and damn well what we saying."

"Rah, shut da fuck up!" I spazzed on him.

"Boy, cut that shit out. And I'm talking 'bout the cheating," Stunna said, slurring his words, and Raheem started laughing.

"Ain't nobody been cheating on shit. Me and Munchie just been going through it over the years. But we gon' get that shit right, and then it's gon' be fuck er'body else," I said, looking at Raheem.

"That's what's up." Raheem nodded.

"What you smirking for? You da main one always in our muthafuckin' business. I'm talking 'bout yo' ass."

"Well, do it then, nigga. Ain't nobody trippin' to be 'round you either. You can believe that." He nodded his head, and something told me to knock his ass out. He might've been drunk, but he was acting real smug about shit, and I didn't like that.

"Y'all stop. Rah, come on and give me a ride back because I know Bishop ain't ready to go," Stunna intervened.

"Yeah, both of y'all get da fuck out my face," I said as they got up.

"Nigga, make sure you take an Uber home. Yo' ass is drunk as fuck." Stunna patted my back before they walked off, and I watched them until they walked out the door.

"What was all that about?" Dula asked, and I turned around to see her in her bottle girl uniform, which was this bikini-looking shit. I was at the bar, and her ass was supposed to be in the club area working.

"Damn, when you walk up?"

"When I came out the bathroom," she said as the bartender brought my shots and placed them in front of me. "I'll help you with that." Dula grabbed one of the shots and tossed it back, and I took the other two without making a face after it hit my chest.

"Ay, baby, lemme get a bottle," I said to the bartender, and she walked away to go get one from the back.

"Damn, look at her already knowing what you want." Dula sucked her teeth and rolled her eyes.

"You jealous?" I asked, spinning around on the stool I was on and pulling her between my legs.

"You drunk as hell." She laughed but didn't bother to step away. She knew me grabbing her the way I did was never some shit I would do in front of people.

"And? Come here," I said, grabbing her face and kissing her soft lips.

She was so damn sexy and loyal to me, and that was what made her the perfect side chick. Plus, she didn't question me when I made her fall back from Munchie's ass, and she wasn't mad when I stopped fucking her. And when I was ready to start back, she didn't have a problem with that either. She knew what having a rich ass nigga like me in her life meant. Somewhere along the lines, Munchie forgot that and started acting like she didn't need me when she knew she did. Her ass was broke as fuck before she met me, so I didn't even understand what she thought she would be without me.

"Here you go, Bishop," the bartender walked back up and said. Dula stepped back, and I spun around on the stool to see the bartender giving me a judgmental stare. She knew I was married, and she already didn't like Dula. But that was because Dula's ass thought she could tell people what to do when I wasn't there, and shawty wasn't going for it.

"Let's go to my office," I whispered in Dula's ear after grabbing my bottle of Don Julio and standing up.

"Lead the way," she said, anxiously and then followed me there.

I already had my pullout bed out and made up because all we did was fuck in there any chance we got. I placed the bottle on my desk while Dula closed the door. I stumbled around a little as I took off my shirt and kicked off my shoes. Then I sat on the bed and lay back with my feet still on the floor. That was a big ass mistake because my head started spinning. I felt Dula climbing on top of me, and I looked up at her and gripped her thighs.

"You my bitch. You know that, don't you?"

"Yes," she said, leaning down to kiss on my neck, and my eyes started to close. "You so drunk." She laughed and sat back up straight, and when I opened my eyes again I saw she had pulled her phone out.

"Da hell you doin'?" I asked slowly.

"I'm texting my sister before I cut this shit off and focus on you for the night."

"Oh, I thought you was tryin' to do sum funny shit like record me and send it to my girl."

"And if I did?" she questioned me.

"I'd kill yo' stupid ass like I did my first baby mama. Give me that shit." I snatched her phone and threw it on the floor. "Now make a nigga feel good," I instructed, and she smiled at me.

"I got you, baby," she said, and I wasn't sure what happened after that, because I was so damn drunk.

❧ 26 ☙

BABY JO
THE NEXT DAY

"Munch, I still can't believe you." I laughed as we got ready to walk out on the beach.

"How the hell was I supposed to know you wasn't talking about Rah? The way you said that shit made it sound like y'all had slept around. Not he took you to meet up with a damn sneaky link." She laughed, fixing the train on my dress as we waited for the music to come on and give the cue to start walking down the aisle, which was really a long white carpet that was laid over the sand.

Munchie, Mary, and my mother had all planned the perfect all-white wedding that I told them I wanted. It was at a venue on the beach, and everything was set up so pretty. The reception was going to be inside, and the wedding was being held on the beach. Bishop was already standing behind Stunna because I wanted Munchie to walk down the aisle with me. I knew she was sick of me because I'd been all over the place all day and nervous as hell. I knew was ready to do this ,but I never expected to be so damn jittery.

"Did you really think Raheem was Sunny's father and I never mentioned it to you? Girl, I wouldn't do no shit like that to you. I just didn't tell anyone because I was ashamed."

"Ashamed? Do you see the situation I'm in?"

"Yeah, I know, but I told myself it was something I would take to the grave with me. Why do you think I was able to leave T-Bank alone and not go back to him after I got out of rehab? Hell, I was hooked on that man. And why do you think I really took them pills? I knew the baby wasn't his and didn't want him to ever find out. That's why I kept trying to push you to tell Bishop the truth before yo' situation got the best of you like it almost did me."

"Jody, I never thought about any of that. I just took your word for what was going on. Damn," she said, getting quiet for a second. "So what pushed you to sleep with someone else?" she asked.

"What do you think? I was tired of his shit and wanted to feel loved for at least one damn night. He made me feel so bad about myself and told me that no one else would want me every single day. So I got on Instagram and slid on another nigga's DM's. It went from there, but once we met up and fucked, I cut him off because I was scared I would get caught. You know they run they mouths like a motherfucker in Jacksonville. I couldn't have that getting out. And before you ask, I know T-Bank isn't her daddy, because the dates didn't add up."

"If no one else feel you, you know I do. And I don't judge you for any of that. You handled the situation a thousand times better than I did."

"Girl, you fucked yo' husband's best friend. You knew better." I laughed.

"And I learned two wrongs sure as hell don't make a right." She smiled at me as the music came on.

"Okay, girls, now," I leaned down and said to Sunny and Ajay, who were back to being the best of friends today. The two of them were going to keep me on my toes for the rest of my damn life. I just knew it. "Wait, slow down," I said after they took off running, throwing flowers any-damn-where.

It wasn't many people in attendance. It was about fifteen

chairs set up, if that many, and all of them were full. Stunna's mother flew into town with her sisters and their kids, and they were the ones who were taking up most of the chairs. Along with them was my mother, Raheem, and Ciara, who was holding Princess.

"You ready to do this, sis?" Munchie asked, looking at me.

"Yes. Thanks for everything, Munch. I love you forever."

"I love you too, Jody."

She looped her arm through mine, and then we started to walk, and everyone turned around to face us as the music switched. But all I could focus on was Stunna's handsome face. The day was finally here, and the shit was feeling surreal. I was actually about to get married, and that was something I never saw happening for me. I had to stop the tears from coming because I felt like I'd accomplished a huge milestone in life.

I found the man who was perfect for me, and I was thankful for him being persistent and Munchie talking some sense into me. If not, I probably would've pulled away from him, but that was something he wasn't willing to let happen. Stunna was simply amazing to sum it up, and he'd taught me a lot. When I couldn't find a good man, that was my cue to switch up my type and give that *lame* or *corny* guy a chance. And honestly, someone good wasn't able to come into my life until after I dropped the baggage and got myself together.

Once I did the work on me, everything else seemed to follow. So I'd learned to focus on myself and better myself, and the rest would come. There would be bumps in the road, but because I had a real man, he rode over them with me instead of turning around and saying fuck it. I was finally happy and couldn't wait to start a lifelong journey with my soon-to-be husband.

"I love you, Mrs. West," Stunna walked up and whispered in my ear as he wrapped his arms around me from behind.

The wedding hadn't been anything short of wonderful, and it was emotional as hell. Stunna started crying as I walked down the aisle, and once I made it to him, I broke down too. The pastor from my mama's church had to wait five whole minutes before he could get started because we were up there smiling and crying like something was wrong with us. Stunna had been through his own problems in life, and I guess he eventually stopped thinking he would find genuine love too. After the way his baby mama did him, I couldn't blame him, but a real woman like me wasn't about to play with that ass.

He was mine, and I was never going to let him go. We wrote our own vows to one another, and that started the crying up all over again, but we managed to get through it. Now the reception had been going for a few hours, and everyone was still partying and getting drunk. The food had been delicious, and no expense had been spared when it came to our big day.

"I love you too, Mr. West," I said, spinning around so I was facing him, and he kissed my lips.

"Come on. It's something I need to do."

"I'll be back, Munchie," I said before allowing Stunna to pull me away. When he walked over to my mother, I was confused.

"This is for you," he said, pulling something out his pocket and passing it to her.

"Oh my goodness. What is all this for, baby?" she asked, looking at both of us, and that was when I realized she was holding a check.

"It's for you a new home," he revealed, and I started cheesing big. That man never ceased to amaze me. And the fact that he would do something like that for my mother meant everything. She'd been staying in the hood for as long as I could remember.

"Are you serious?" she asked and started to tear up.

"Yeah. Get you something nice for you and the girls when they come over," he said, giving her a hug, and she nodded her head. "But I have one request, and it's completely up to you," he added.

"Yes?"

"Can you wait until my wife gets her GED and real estate license and then buy the property from her?" he questioned, and I looked at him in awe.

After doing so good with renting out my own condo, it made me want to try my hand at something a little bigger, and that was real estate. But since I'd ran away from home at the age of sixteen, I never got the chance to graduate from high school. So my GED was my first goal, and then I was going after my real estate license. I might've been married to a billionaire who I could always trust to be there, but making my own money was still a must for me, as well as setting goals and reaching them because although I'd done a lot of work on myself, I was nowhere near finished. When it came to that, I felt like it was always something that could be improved. Or maybe it was the grind and determination that had always been in me. Either way, I was going for it, pregnant and all.

"Jo Jo, you getting your GED and going after a real estate license?" my mama asked. I nodded. "That's amazing, sweetie. I know I tell you this all the time, and you may be sick of hearing it, but I am so damn proud of you."

"Mama!" I yelled, surprised she'd cursed.

"What? I had to let you know how proud of you I am. God knows my heart." She smiled and rubbed my arm.

It was obvious why she'd hit it off with Stunna's mama from the jump. They were alike in many ways, and although today was their first time meeting in person, no one would've been able to tell. Mary being a woman of God also explained why Stunna didn't end up going down the same road as Raheem and Bishop. And he didn't even know who the hell T-Bank was, although they'd grown up in the same city. Stunna's path had been different, and I was glad because it made him a humble and loving man.

"Thanks, Ma. I'll never get tired of hearing that. So what do you say? You gon' let me sell you your first mansion?" I asked, smiling.

"Of course. I wouldn't want it any other way," she said and hugged me.

"But..." Stunna said, and we turned to look at him.

"What now?" I giggled.

"Jody will be licensed in Nevada."

"Are you asking me to move to Vegas?" she questioned, and her eyes lit up.

"Yes, Mama. We are." I looked down at her because she was shorter than me.

"I don't know what to say." She looked around.

"Don't miss ya blessing nii," Stunna joked, and I hit his arm. He always had to start with his antics. My mama laughed, and then she looked from me to him.

"I would love to. This means the world to me," she said, tearing up, and I hugged her again and rubbed her back.

"And rebuilding my bond with you has meant the world to me. Just know that I forgive you for the past, and from this moment on, we'll never look back." I kissed her forehead and then pulled away to see the tears rolling down her cheeks.

"Thank you, baby. That's all I ever wanted and needed. Won't God do it!" she shouted, throwing her hands in the air. "He's able!" She carried on.

"He most definitely will." I chuckled and wiped her tears away.

"Ouu! Wait until Sunday! I can't wait to tell my testimony to Pastor," she said, shaking her head and rocking a little like a true church lady. I smiled, and she hugged Stunna again before rushing off to go find Mary.

"You know our mamas 'bout to tear that church up in Nevada, right?" Stunna questioned, and I busted out laughing.

"Baby, you better believe it. And who is that talking to Ciara?" I pointed across the room, and Stunna looked.

"Oh, that's my cousin C-Mo. He probably tryin' to holler at her knowing that lil' nigga."

"C-Mo? What kind of name is that, and how old is he?"

"Eighteen, and he say they call him C-Mo 'cause he see mo' money than a lot of these niggas." Stunna started cracking up, but I didn't find anything funny.

"Is he in the streets?"

"That nigga in the streets, beds, robberies, and everything else. Matter fact, you might wanna go break that shit up."

I didn't even respond to him. I marched straight over to where they was standing and didn't say anything. I wanted to hear what he was saying to her first because it might've just been a casual conversation, although I highly doubted that from the way they was grinning at each other.

"So that's yo' baby I been seeing you wit' all day?" C-Mo asked with his head cocked back a little.

He was tall as hell and light skin with a temp fade and curly hair. Along with the tattoos I saw creeping up his neck and on his hands, that was a recipe for heartbreak and a whole lot of bullshit. Not saying she didn't deserve a nice-looking guy though. Ciara wasn't a nerd, but she most definitely looked like one. She was too nice of a girl to get involved with some young thug. Nope. That shit wasn't happening on my watch. Maybe I was overreacting, but I knew how that shit was gon' go.

"No, I'm her babysitter." She giggled, and pushed her glasses up on her face.

"Word? You ain't got no kids?"

"No, I'm only eighteen, and I've been helping my mama raise my siblings for years. That was all the birth control I needed."

"So I'm da same age and got three... two lil' boys and a girl. They got different mamas, but you know how that shit be." He shrugged like it was nothing.

"No, she don't *know how that shit be*," I interrupted, mocking him while moving my shoulders like he did.

"Oh, what's up, fam?" he asked, excitedly. "Ciara, I'ma hit you up later. You better answer da phone too," he said like he was cool and escaped before I could get on his ass.

"Delete his number."

"I don't have it... I gave him mine," she said innocently, and I knew she was falling for the charm because she was blushing.

"Well, when he call, block him. You don't need those problems in your life. You hear me?" I asked, and she nodded. "I'm serious."

"I will," she said and walked off, not even knowing what she'd been saved from. At times, I wished someone would've done the same for me, but then, I would've never met Stunna.

"Jody!" Munchie yelled, walking over to me dancing, and I didn't hesitate to join in.

The rest of the reception flew by, and at the end of the night, everyone watched as Stunna and I left for our honeymoon. I was grateful and humble because my story could've ended a thousand other ways.

27

BISHOP

TWO WEEKS LATER

"Munchie!" I stood at the bottom of the stairs and yelled with my hand up to the side of my mouth.

"What, Bishop!" she hollered, but I still didn't see her appear at the top of the stairs and blew out a frustrated breath.

"We gon' be late for our own anniversary party if we don't leave now. Bring yo' ass on!"

"I'm coming!" she screamed like I was irritating her or something.

She'd been acting stupid all motherfucking week, and it was like she didn't even care to have the party. I knew the shit was my plan, but we had an agreement, and as far as she knew, I hadn't stepped out on her or nothing. I'd been the perfect gentleman to her ass other than when I didn't come home after Stunna's bachelor party. That shit wasn't my fault though, because after I passed out, I didn't wake up until early that next morning. Dula was gone, and I couldn't remember a thing, so I figured it had been a wild night. It really didn't matter, because Munchie didn't seem to know that I never returned home that night. Or she just didn't give a fuck... one.

"Ciara, you call me if you need me, okay?" Munchie asked as she and Ciara finally appeared at the top of the stairs.

"I will," Ciara said. She had Princess, who was still wide awake, situated on her hip. She was the reason my baby was spoiled now because she always wanted to hold her.

"This ain't her first time staying the night and watching her, Munchie. She know what to do and how to get in touch with us. Come da fuck on," I said, getting impatient.

"Jo, I'ma have to call you later," she said, suddenly looking at her phone, and that was when I realized her ass was on Face-Time too.

Was she serious?

"Wait, look at these earrings I got!" I heard Jody yelling.

"Now if I come drag yo' ass down them steps and have yo' head knocking on them the whole way down, I'ma be fucking wrong."

"Shut up!"

"Whooo?"

"Those are cute as hell. I can't believe y'all was in the Bahamas last week and in Paris now. Y'all ain't playing 'bout this honeymoon." Munchie laughed, and that was when I realized she was still talking to Jody and ignoring me.

"Munchie!"

"Girl, let me go before this man blow a damn gasket with his crazy ass." She rolled her eyes.

"Yeah, you made me fucking crazy," I mumbled under my breath. I was crazy before I met her, but somehow she'd managed to make me even crazier with her constant bullshit. She was really about to piss me off because if she didn't want to do the damn party, she should've told me so I could've come up with something else. I wouldn't have had no problem with that.

"Bye, Ciara, and I know you just got yo' new car. Don't go taking my baby nowhere. I don't care if it's the store."

"I know." Ciara laughed.

"Unless somebody give you permission," I added, and Munchie looked at me funny like I was going against what she said. She shook her head and then kissed Princess. My daughter was so beautiful, and she looked more like Bella than she did BJ, as crazy as that was.

Munchie finally made her way downstairs, and I was able to get a good look at her. She looked sexy as hell in a sparkling gray dress that her titties was spilling out of. It had long sleeves and stopped right above her knees. Her earrings looked like chains, and she had her hair pulled to the side and pinned. Her makeup was done, and I watched as she dabbed some of her red lipstick off with the tissue she'd been holding.

"What?" Munchie asked, noticing me staring at her.

"You lookin' casket sharp," I complimented, but the look on her face said she didn't take it as that.

"What you mean?" She placed her hand on her hip.

"Baby, it's a compliment, damn. Can we go?" I questioned, and she rolled her eyes before finally walking out the house with me right behind her.

We walked inside the ballroom at the hotel we were having the party at, and Munchie seemed surprised to see so many people. I'd invited a few people I did business with, the whole hood, and anybody else I thought wanted to come. I wanted it packed as we could get it for our celebration, and everyone had come through for me by showing up. We walked inside, and I saw Raheem was already present. Of course he would be though. That nigga didn't want to miss shit that was going on with me and Munchie.

"Damn, I ain't think y'all was gon' make it," he said, and we slapped hands. We were being fake as fuck, and I knew he knew that. But it was a certain way I had to play shit when it came to a nigga who stayed getting involved in some shit he ain't have no business in.

"Who is all these people, Bishop?" Munchie looked at me and ignored Raheem. I guess they were mad at each other. That was real cute being that they stayed in one another's fucking face.

"These my people. They wanted to help *us* celebrate *our* anniversary." I smirked at Raheem. I wanted everyone to witness our special night.

"I guess," she said and looked at the crowd again.

"Come on." I grabbed her hand and walked off from Raheem, and I could've sworn I saw the nigga bite down on his lip like that pissed him off. I grabbed Munchie's coat she'd been holding in her hands and took mine off to pass to a guy working at our event so he could put them up somewhere.

For the first hour, we ate and talked with our guests, and then after that, the bar opened up, and the music got started. I made sure to keep Munchie by my side the whole entire time, and before I knew it a couple of hours had passed by. I wasn't sure where the hell Raheem kept going, but every time I would start looking for him again, I would spot him in the corner watching our every move. The nigga clearly felt some type of way, but I had a toast to make and wasn't tripping off him.

"Here's the microphone, sir," one of the workers walked up to me and said, and I grabbed the mic.

"'Preciate that," I said, and then he walked off. "'Scuse me. Can I get everyone's attention?" I asked, and the DJ turned the music down. Everyone started facing the front where Munchie and I were standing. "I want to make a toast, and it should be someone coming around with the wine now. Just grab a glass, and once everybody got theirs, I'll make the toast."

"Bishop," Munchie hissed, but before I could answer her a woman walked up and passed us our wine glasses. I waited for a few minutes longer to make sure everyone had their drinks, and then I put the mic up to my mouth and cleared my throat.

"I want to thank everybody for coming out tonight and cele-brating me and my beautiful wife's five-year anniversary. What didn't kill us only made us stronger, and I have this woman to praise for that. You a nigga's rib, my heartbeat, the mother of my kids, and my motivation. Without you, I don't know where I'd be today," I said, raising my glass to the crowd in front of us as I looked at Munchie. She smiled and did the same. Then we clinked our glasses together and took a sip of the wine. "I love you," I leaned over and whispered in her ear.

"I love you too," she whispered back and then got silent as she stared off into space.

"You good, baby?" I placed my hand on the small of her back.

"No, I think I'm ready to leave," she admitted, and I wasn't surprised. Munchie was still having her days, and sometimes certain shit would be too much for her, so I guess the party was one of those things, especially being that today made a year since we lost BJ.

"Let me grab our coats and say goodbye," I said, but she shook her head.

"There's no need for both of us to leave. I thought I could get through the night and celebrate with you, but it's too much." She shook her head again as tears started to build up in her eyes.

"I understand. You already know you ain't got to explain shit, Munchie." I placed my glass down on the table that was next to us and then took her glass from her and placed it down as well. I wrapped her up in my arms and held her tight for a second. "Everything I do is for us. Remember that," I said before letting her go.

"I know, baby," she said, cupping the side of my face.

"Should I get someone to drive you home?" I asked, and she quickly shook her head.

"Ay, Bishop!" Raheem yelled, approaching us.

"Hol' on, baby. I'll get Rah to take you home right fast. I can tell you out of it, and I'm not about to let you drive like this," I said, stopping her dead in her tracks because she was trying to walk away.

"I'm fine, baby. Trust me. I need the time alone."

"Nah," I said dismissively and then leaned over to whisper to Raheem so her nosy ass couldn't hear me. "Ay, you think you can take Munchie home right fast? She ain't feeling too good."

"You cool wit' me doin' that? You seem like you done had sumthin' on yo' chest all night."

"Nah, I'm straight. You got sumthin' on yo' chest?"

"Man, I'll be back," he said, ignoring my question.

"You sure it's worth it?" I asked, looking at him funny.

"Shit, I don't mind," he said, and I nodded before patting him on the back and walking away.

"I bet you don't, motherfucker," I said as soon as I saw him walk out with Munchie not too far behind him. I looked around the room and then walked to a corner and pulled my phone out. I dialed a number and waited while the phone rang.

"Hello?"

"Ciara, I need you to bring Princess to the party now. I'll send you the address, and when you get here sit in the lobby and wait for me," I instructed.

"What's going on?"

"Nothing. Just hurry up and do it now." I hung up and sent her the address before looking around the room and then stepping to one of my workers. "Ay, bruh, let me get yo' hoodie." He didn't ask any questions and pulled it off and passed it to me. I put it on right there over the suit I was wearing and then pulled the hood on my head. "Anybody start looking for me, tell them my babysitter had an emergency and had to come drop my daughter off."

"I got you," he said, and I dapped him up before slipping out an emergency exit door unnoticed. Usually, that door would've set off an alarm as soon as I opened it, but I knew someone who worked at the hotel and already had that shit fixed for me, which was the reason I chose the hotel to start with. I didn't give a damn about it being luxurious. It was always about connections. I stood outside and looked down at my phone, and before I could send another text, I saw my car pulling up to the back, and the guy who worked at the hotel jumped out, leaving it running.

"Everything good to go. All I have to do is get my person in security to shut the system down and act like we lost all the footage from tonight."

"Bet," I said, slapping hands with him. "Check your account in two weeks and not a day before."

"Cool. Thanks, man."

"Nah, thank you," I said and then went to jump in my ride before easing out of the parking lot.

Once I made it onto the highway, I stepped on the gas. About twenty-five minutes later, Ciara was texting me and telling me that she was in the lobby, but I didn't respond. I told her ass to sit there and wait for me, and I hoped she knew how to follow instructions. I didn't need her fucking up my plans for the night. Everything had to be done just right. It wasn't any room for error. But as long as she had my baby safe and out of the way, I was good to go.

When I finally neared my estate, I pulled on the side of the road in a dark spot and waited. A minute later, I saw Raheem pulling out as expected, and once he got down the road, I sprang into action. I moved from the side and turned into my driveway. I didn't have to worry about putting a damn code in, because the gate had been left open, and that told me everything I needed to know. Munchie was about to try to run, but I had a trick for that bitch.

The charade was over, and it was go time. I parked in front of the mansion and then leaped out after grabbing my gun from under the seat. As soon as I got to the door, I lifted my foot and kicked the hell out of it. I stomped inside, and a few seconds later, I saw Munchie coming down the stairs. I aimed my gun at her, and she looked like she saw a ghost as soon as she got to the bottom.

"Bishop, what's going on?" she asked, holding her trembling hands up.

"You tell me, bitch."

"What you talking about? I wanted to come home and go to bed, and when I got here Princess and Ciara was gone. Why did you tell her to bring Princess to the party?" she asked, trying to act like she didn't know what the fuck was going on, but her eyes said something differently. I'd taught her how to read body language, but ever since she decided she wanted to be done with the streets, she started to slack in a lot of areas. Maybe if she was on her toes, she would've seen the shit coming to her at the beginning of the damn night.

"How long?"

"How long what?"

"How fucking long!" I roared, and her bottom lip started to quiver.

"I don't know what you're talking about," her voice cracked.

"I'll tell you how long. Three fucking years."

"Bishop," she said, trying to take a step toward me.

"Don't you make a motherfucking move. You gots to be the dumbest, most low-down bitch I have ever met in my fucking life. You and Raheem? Really? That's some fucked-up ass shit. I might could've respected yo' get-back game if it wasn't wit' my so-called best friend."

"I don't have anything going on with Rah."

"Lie again! See, you always thought you was a step ahead of me. but bitch. I been ten steps ahead of y'all since BJ turned one." Her eyes widened. and I smirked at her. "You really thought I passed out and forgot shit? I woke up as soon as Baby Jo and Stunna left in that noisy ass car. I knew Raheem was still there. so I faked like I was knocked the hell out. You see, I caught on to you two motherfuckers a long time ago. You remember that day you ran past Raheem's kitchen? Yeah, you ain't think I would recognize you. did you? Bitch. my hands and tongue been all over yo' fucking body. I know what you shaped liked. and when Raheem said that dumbass shit about it being another nigga's wife, I knew it was you for sure."

"Bishop."

"I'm not fucking done!" I walked over to her and grabbed her by the throat and placed the gun to her head. "You gon' die tonight. bitch. But before you do. it's a lot more you should know. When I got home that day. it took a lot in me not to put a bullet in your head. Then you told me you was pregnant. and that saved yo' hoe ass. After seeing you at Raheem's place. I knew it was a chance that BJ couldn't be mine. So I purposely made you name him after me to see how far you was willing to drag that damn lie. I'ma give it to y'all though. Y'all was playing that shit out to the best of your abilities. But did you ever ask yourself why I made you stay in the streets, knowing you was pregnant? I didn't give a fuck about you or that bastard ass baby in ya stomach. And after BJ was born and only looked like you, I knew what was up. That wasn't what did it though. It was his skin tone. I'm black as fuck, and you not that light ya-damn-self. So why da fuck was our baby yellow? Huh?"

"I'm sorry," she started to cry, and I smiled at her wickedly.

"You not sorry yet. Because even when I suspected all of that, I wasn't a thousand percent sure until that night on the couch when I heard you and Raheem talking about BJ being his. You tried to make him hush, but I'd already heard everything I needed to hear. And when you walked that nigga out, I sat straight the hell up on that couch and waited for you to come back. That nigga Rah thought he had you on lock, and while I was grieving the death of my baby, you two motherfuckers was laid up in that house he bought you. See, you not as smart as you think you is. And when I broke down, that was my true feelings. I just didn't expect you to actually be there for me, and once you was I knew I was going to fuck you. I knew I had to get you pregnant with my baby because in my head, that would be enough to break you motherfuckers up. But it wasn't, and y'all continued to fuck around."

I stopped talking and just looked at her. She was pathetic to me, and she didn't even know what to say. She was visibly shaking, and that shit made my dick hard. I wanted her to be scared. I wanted her to see what the fuck she'd caused, and she hadn't even heard the best part yet.

"Please... just let me go," she begged, and I slapped her across the face with my gun. Her knees buckled, and I removed my hand from her throat. She fell to the ground and started sobbing louder, but that didn't move me. I squatted down next to her and grabbed a handful of her hair roughly.

"Nah, don't break down yet. You ain't even heard the best part." I laughed.

"Get off me!" she yelled and tried to buck at me, swinging her arms wildly.

Wap! Wap! Wap! I punched her upside her fat ass head three times, and that took the buck right out of her. There was no need to try to fight, because I'd already told her she wasn't making it out of this shit alive, and I meant that.

"I actually loved you, bitch. I knew I fucked up with Rissa, and I regretted that shit and was willing to actually try to make it work. But no, you just had to go and fuck Raheem behind my back. Now ask me what's the best part." I grinned, and she shook her head. "Ask me!"

"Oh, God," she cried.

"No need to call on Him. I'm pretty sure He said fuck you when he saw how big of a deceiving ass hoe you was. Now ask me." I stuck the gun under her nose that had snot running out of it. She looked a fucking mess.

"You fucking sick! You a sick ass psycho! If you been knew, why did you wait all this time?"

"You been knew I was fucked up in the head since day one. And why did I wait? Because I was going to make you two motherfuckers pay in the worst way. I needed you to suffer the same way I did and still have been. I wanted you to actually think you had a chance, and right when shit seemed sweet, I slid in like the grim reaper himself and took yo' fucking son's life. Yeah..." I nodded my head. "That was all me, and I put that shit on that bracelet and waited for you to connect the gah damn dots. When you did, I went to the next phase and planned this day out perfectly. Yo' son dead just like my daughter, bitch. And I should've chose Rissa over you. At least she had some damn loyalty. You and Raheem played the game, but I played it even better. That's right, cry, but it won't bring yo' son back, and if I could, I would kill his ass all over again," I said and then heard someone at the door. I quickly jumped up and aimed my gun at Raheem, who was aiming his gun at me.

❧ 28 ❧

RAHEEM

I stood with my gun pointed at Bishop, and my jaw clenched. When I left, I got exactly ten minutes away before I turned around and raced back to the estate. It hit me at the party that he was really on to us when he asked me if it was worth it. He wasn't talking about me giving Munchie a ride home. He was talking about her period. He wanted to know if she was worth fucking up our friendship, and she sure as hell was, but I played dumb so I could get Munchie out of there.

On my way home, I realized everything was a set up and Bishop would never give us time to get away. I figured he left out right after us, and that was why I turned around and raced back. When I pulled up, I knew I was right because his car was out front. I parked and jumped out of mine and didn't bother to close the door. I ran up the steps, and when I neared the front door, I heard that nigga admitting to killing my son, so there we were, staring at each other with hateful eyes. But the hate inside me for Bishop had been there long before we ever met Munchie.

"Look, bitch, it's yo' knight and shining fuck nigga," Bishop said, pointing his gun back at Munchie. "Get da fuck up," he said, and she struggled to get up from the floor. Her face was bloody and clearly swelling the hell up. "I wouldn't do that, or this bitch gon' die too," Bishop warned, noticing me about to pull the trigger. He snatched Munchie in front of him and put the gun up to her head.

"Let her go," I said calmly. "And we can handle shit just me and you."

"I ain't got shit to say to you, nigga, but I took yo' fuckin' son out just like I'ma do to you. Every fucking day, you stared me in the face, knowing you was fucking my bitch behind my back. Shit like that makes me want to kill a nigga slowly after making him suffer time and time again for years. I know it must've sucked to watch me all on her. It sucked to watch your son be named after another nigga. Oh, and I can't forget, it sucked to see yo' bitch get pregnant by another nigga, huh? Well, now you know exactly how I felt when I found out BJ wasn't mine. I hope yo' fucking heart caved in when she told you she was going to have my baby. See, the thing about get back is you have to know what the hell you doing. Every move has to be calculated before it's made, and every lie has to be precise before it's told. You two was never a match for me, you fucking idiots! And for a while, I couldn't believe you would cross me over a bitch. Shit, I can't believe you crossed me at all."

"Like you crossed me?" I asked, and he started to look confused.

"I ain't never crossed you, nigga!" he yelled.

"That's a gah damn lie! You killed both of my fucking parents over drug money when we was only seventeen. I was there, and I saw you do it, even though you didn't see me. I told myself for the longest that you ain't know who they was. How could you when the only person you'd ever saw was my grandma? You was young, reckless, and hurt about yo' people. That shit was something you was never able to get over, and it ruined you, nigga. It fucked yo' head up, and I felt bad for you. Even after I found out the truth that you knew exactly who my people was when you killed them, I still tried to convince myself otherwise. Ever since that day, I knew you wasn't a motherfucker who deserved my loyalty, but by then, millions of dollars was involved, and I would've been a fool to walk away or kill the person who had all the connects. I hated my parents anyway for the way they did me, but it was about the fucking principle!"

"Okay, yeah, I did it. Cry about it, bitch. Fuck you and yo' junky ass parents. You was always carrying on about hating them crackheads, so how the fuck was I supposed to know you would give a damn?"

"Why wouldn't I!" I yelled, and spit flew out of my mouth. "They birthed me! Just because I hated them didn't mean I wanted them to die at the hands of a nigga who was supposed to have my back!"

"Damn, Munchie, this nigga used you to get back at me for some shit that happened years and years ago." He laughed, and Munchie started to truly look hurt, but that was never the case.

"I ain't use her for a gah damn thing. She came to me crying about you getting that thot ass girl pregnant. You couldn't make her feel good, so I did. I just never expected to fall for her, but when I did, I didn't hold back. I ain't owe you no fucking loyalty, so I went after what I wanted, and I got her. Why would I use this as revenge when I could've been got at you! You a delusional ass nigga. Can't even trust shit you say, because it's all been a lie. At least Munchie and I knew we was lying, but at some point, I think you really started to convince yourself of the damn lies you was telling. Only a twisted ass nigga could do the shit you done pulled over the last few years. You was never the nigga for her, and you could never love her because you've always been heartless. This we both know." We were so busy going back and forth arguing that we didn't even hear the numerous footsteps running up the stairs.

"Police! Police!"

We heard yelling, and Bishop pushed Munchie away from him. I quickly tucked my gun in my jeans and grabbed Munchie, who started crying uncontrollably. She wasn't a pawn. She was my fucking heart that I went after when the chance presented itself. Our relationship never had a thing to do with me getting back at Bishop, but I didn't know if she would ever believe that.

"What da fuck?" I asked as they stormed in the house and aimed their guns at Bishop, who now had his gun aimed at them.

"Drop the weapon! Bishop King Sr., you are under arrest for the kidnapping of Bishop King Jr. and the murder of Marissa Greene," an officer said, and everything seemed to stop. Bishop's whole facial expression changed, and it seemed like he came to the realization that he was about to go to jail for life.

"Drop the weapon!" another officer yelled, and Bishop looked over at us with a weird ass expression on his face that sent chills through me, and Munchie must've felt it too because she shivered.

"I'll see you two muthafuckas in hell," he said, and his eyes went dark.

"Oh, God!" Munchie screamed as he placed the gun up to his head.

"Wait!" the officer yelled, but it was too late.

Pow!

MUNCHIE
TWO WEEKS LATER

Two weeks passed by, and that was hardly enough time for me to catch my breath after everything that'd taken place. I couldn't wrap my mind around any of it for that first week. Then there was Bishop's funeral I had to plan since I was still his wife. I didn't want to do it, and cremation crossed my mind over and over again. Two wrongs didn't make a right, and three were a recipe for disaster.

That was exactly what Bishop's funeral was because when Brandy showed up, all hell broke loose. She wasn't happy to see me or Raheem, and she flipped out and started yelling everything was our fault and that we was the ones who had killed him. I was just sitting there watching her go off when she slapped the shit out of me and punched me in the mouth. It happened so fast I didn't even know it happened until after. I didn't try to fight her back though, because that wasn't the reason I was there.

Brandy had a right to feel the way she did, and I wouldn't deny that, but if she wanted to point the finger at us, she had to look at the one pointing back at her. She'd repeatedly tossed him to the side and was never there when he needed her. So part of that blame, she could hold. Anyway, after the funeral, things didn't get any better. As rich as Bishop was, I would've thought that he'd come up with a will with his lawyer, but that wasn't the case.

He didn't have one, and when his lawyer announced that information, Brandy was the first one to jump up and say everything belonged to her. That entitlement ended quickly because the lawyer said it all belonged to me since I was his wife. She tried to attack me again, but Jody was quick to get up and stop her in her tracks. She told Brandy she understood she was hurting, but it was best if she sat the fuck down. And like Jody said, she sat the fuck down.

Jody hadn't attended the funeral, but she did show up for me after that fact. I couldn't say I blamed her, because I didn't. Once the truth came out about him definitely being the one to kill Rissa, she was done. In the end, I gave Brandy the estate because that wasn't a place I ever wanted to see again, or her, and she felt the same way about me. It was what it was. She had the right to feel how she wanted, and so did I. Thankfully, I already got through all that, but it was still a few more things I needed to know and hear for myself.

"You sure you want to do this?" Raheem walked in the kitchen and asked.

For the first couple days after everything happened, I didn't talk to him. I just needed time to myself. But eventually, I allowed him to come over to the house he bought for me, and we talked things out. He explained everything to me, and basically, he didn't feel like he owed Bishop any loyalty. Not saying what we did was right, but everyone had fucked up somewhere along the lines. And after Bishop confessed to seeing me at Raheem's house that day, everything he did after that finally made sense. He didn't give a fuck about me, and I would rather he had confronted us before everything went down the way it did.

"Yes. I'm going to that fucking jail, and that bitch is going to tell me everything the police already told me and more." I slammed the orange juice I'd grabbed out the fridge down on the counter.

"Mommy! Mommy!" BJ yelled, and I smiled as I walked over to him at Raheem's kitchen table.

My baby was two going on three this year, and it was crazy that I was even able to say that. Everything inside me had been healed when he returned, and he was the reason why I couldn't sympathize with what happened to Bishop. Although I felt the image of him shooting himself would always haunt Raheem and me both, knowing we played our part in things getting to that point, it was something we would have to live with.

"Yes, sweetie?" I asked, wrapping an arm around him.

"Juice." He pointed, and I grabbed his cup and went to put some orange juice in it.

"Can you feed Princess for me?" I looked at Raheem.

"I'm already on it," he said, going to grab her baby food. She was next to the table sitting in her high chair and looking at the TV in the kitchen that was playing cartoons.

"I love y'all so much. I'll be back," I said, placing BJ's cup on the table for him as he ate his breakfast with his hands. I gave him a tight hug and kiss and then walked over to Princess "Bye, baby girl." I tickled her and kissed her cheek.

"We love you too," Raheem said. "And if you need me for anything or don't think you can drive home, just call, and me and the kids will be on the way."

"Okay," I agreed and gave him a kiss on the lips before heading out.

⚜

"I didn't think you would come," Dula said after picking the phone up and looking at me through the glass. "Thank you," she said softly.

"I'm here to ask one thing only... Why?" I stared at her because it was something that I needed to know.

"I really am sorry, Munchie," she sighed, running a hand through her hair.

"Just tell me!" I yelled, hitting the table in front of me.

"Bishop and I where scheming from the jump. That's what our relationship started off as... business. When he ran into me at the strip club, I gave him my number to give to you before he left. And then you never called me. But one day, he did, and he said he had a way for me to make some money. I was in a fucked-up position at the time, so I took the offer."

"And what did you have to do?"

"I had to come to the grand opening at the casino and befriend you. After that, my job was to simply watch you and report everything to Bishop. And I did. I never wanted to cross you, but I wasn't about to pass up easy money. I couldn't afford to do that."

"Dula, I don't give a fuck about that. Skip to what I really want to know."

"We started messing around with one another off and on because, as you know, I was working at the casino. And one day, he called me into his office and said he needed for me to do something for him and that he would pay me five hundred thousand dollars," she said, and I swallowed hard. "I asked him what he needed for me to do, and he said he wanted me to kill BJ. I told him I couldn't do no shit like that, and he lost his fucking mind, but he raised the pay to a million dollars and said all I had to do was lock him in a room and starve him to death. And before you judge me, do you know what I was able to do with that money?"

"Bitch, I don't give a damn. What happened after that?" I questioned, even though my stomach already dropped.

"I agreed to do it, and he said everything would go down on your four-year anniversary. So when that day came, he gave me the address to where BJ was at and told me to park across the street and wait until I seen him pulling off with BJ to get behind him. I did exactly that and followed him down a secluded road.

That's where we both got out, and he gave me BJ, who was asleep. I laid him in my back seat and watched as Bishop shot his own car up. He never called the police, because there was never a drive-by. It was all him, Munchie. He faked like he went to the hospital, and a couple days later, he went out and bought an urn and put fake ashes in it. That's why he lied like no one could see BJ's body because he had to do that. But he's not a bad person, because he honestly couldn't kill BJ himself, regardless of how mad he was."

"Are you fucking crazy? He paid you to kill BJ for him. It doesn't matter if he did it or not. He wanted my baby dead," I choked up. "And for a whole fucking year, I believed he was!"

"Well, Bishop honestly thought he was dead too because I told him he was a few days later. But the truth is, I couldn't follow through with the plan. When I got home that night with him in the back seat he woke up and started crying. Then he saw my face and calmed down because I guess he was used to me always hanging out with you. And I don't know... He must've been confused because he'd just woke up, but he called me mama. That's when it hit me that was the only time I would ever hear those words. So I got him out my back seat and went inside. I gave him a bath and then took him to bed with me, and from that night on, I finally was a mother. I know you might hate me, but Munchie, I took care of him for a whole year. I saved his life and kept the truth away from Bishop. He never came to my house anyway because we always fucked at the casino. So I did the right thing. I did you a favor, and that should count for something," she had the audacity to say.

"You ain't do shit. If you wanted to do the right thing, you would've called me and told me what was going on the same day Bishop offered you the money to kill my son or brought him to *me*. Instead, you wanted to play like he was your son. That's why you really stopped coming around me because you had him. I was so fucking stupid, and I should've listened to Jody about you.

If your sister hadn't popped up at your house and saw him, none of this would even be happening right now."

"Yeah, you're right. She popped up, and I was trying to get him to stop crying, but he wouldn't, and she heard him. She came into my room, and when she saw him she started questioning me about whose child I had, and then she realized it was the little boy I would take my nephew to go play with. So I had to confess everything and told her it was my chance to be a mother. I begged that bitch not to ruin shit for me, and what did she do? Lie. She told me I could trust her just for her to drive straight to the fucking police station and report me. They came and kicked my damn door down and said I was under arrest. That's when I tried to show them the video I recorded of Bishop saying he killed his first baby mama. It was supposed to be blackmail just in case he ever found out the truth about BJ and tried to take him from me, but I still got locked the fuck up, and I guess they came to his house next." She shrugged, and if I could've beat her ass through that glass, I would've.

But that was exactly what I needed to know to move on from what happened. I didn't know who was fucking sicker—her or Bishop. Then again, she could've killed my baby, and I was just glad that she didn't. Yet I would never forgive her. I stood up, still holding the phone and looked directly at her through the glass.

"How much time are you getting?" I asked.

"I don't know yet."

"Well, I'll tell you this. If you ever step foot out into the real world again, I'ma be the first person you see," I said and dropped the phone and left.

EPILOGUE
MUNCHIE

TWO YEARS LATER

"Congratulations on the new home and engagement, babe," Jody said as she wobbled through the door, looking like Clifford the big red dog. For one, she had on all red, and two, she was big as hell, but she was glowing and looking better than ever before.

"No, congratulations to you on the triplets," I said, rubbing her belly.

"Munch, cut it out cuz you know when I first found out, that shit had me crying all motherfucking night," she joked, and I bet it did because I would have been the same way.

"What's up! What's up nii!" Stunna said, walking through the door with Sunny, Ajay, and Mecca alongside him. Turned out, Jody was pregnant with a boy when they got married, and they were so happy when they found out. Now she was knocked up again with two boys and a girl.

"Hey, Aunt Munchie," the girls said in unison, and I leaned down to give them a hug as they walked over to me.

"Hey, girls. Hey, Mecca." I said, and he smiled and waved, holding on to his daddy's leg. He was a little shy and had the chunkiest cheeks that made me want to pinch them. He looked more like Stunna than Jody.

The kids took off running to go play with Ryland, whose name had been changed from BJ for obvious reasons, and Princess. Stunna and Jody were doing everything they set out to do. Jody was a successful real estate agent now, and she was killing the sales, pregnant and all. I already knew Stunna was going to make her sit down for a few months after she had the kids, and she wasn't going to like that at all. Stunna was still making money and opening casinos anywhere he thought about throwing one up at.

Raheem and I were doing a pretty good job running ours. Since everything was left to me after Bishop died, I became part owner, and I was currently taking classes to get a degree in business management with a push from Jody.

"Hey, Stunna," I finally said, and he gave me a side hug.

"Where can I put the housewarming gift at? These niggas say they done built a whole ass beach house on the beach," Stunna said, and I laughed.

"Over there on the table, and where else would we build a beach house at?" I asked, and Jody started laughing.

"That part," she said, and Stunna slapped her ass.

"Leave me alone. My boy! Where you at, fool?" he asked and walked away from us, and we continued to laugh at him because he was still goofy as hell.

"Come out here and smoke one wit' me!" Raheem stuck his head through the patio door that was open and said.

"Damn, you can see the ocean from y'all living room and all. Oh, this shit is *nice, nice*," Jody said.

"Thanks, boo. Come on. Let's go sit down."

"That would be helpful," she said, holding on to her back, and we made our way to the sectional and took a seat.

"So how does it feel now that the adoption is finally finalized?" I asked.

"It feels real good. The guy I had the one-night stand with

was definitely her father, and after we found him and called him up, he agreed to meet with us. At first, I thought he was going to give us some problems, but that nigga was married and didn't want the truth getting out. He signed them papers with the quickness."

"I'm so glad y'all was able to get everything situated."

"You and me both."

It took two years for Stunna and Jody to finally be able to adopt each other's daughter, and now that they had, I knew they felt complete. I was happy for Ajay too because her biological mama died in a car accident last year, but she didn't even really know her. Jody said she never asked anything about her mama after Stunna explained what was going on. To Ajay, Jody was the only mother she had, but Stunna made sure to stay transparent with her because he didn't want to keep anything from her.

T-Bank ended up getting sentenced to life in prison because apparently, he had warrants along with the charges he'd racked up when he pulled that dumb shit at Jody's condo. So she wouldn't have to worry about him popping up and finding out that Sunny wasn't his child after all. As expected, his mother went on with her miserable life, and Jody hadn't heard from or seen her since that day at the hospital. So life was going pretty damn good for them after their wedding, and they deserved that.

"I'ma let you give birth first, and then we gon' start planning my wedding," I said, and Jody nodded.

"I'm ready now. Fuck that. I knew Rah wasn't going to wait too long before he popped that question," she said, and I couldn't help but cheese.

Raheem proposed to me a few weeks ago while we was on vacation with the kids at the resort he owned. After Bishop killed himself, there was no point in us moving out of the country. So we visited the resort often, and it had been successful as hell so far. We were bringing in millions and doing it without drugs. Raheem didn't hesitate to let all of that shit go and step away from that lifestyle, even when the plug reached out to him and still wanted to do business. He found out what Bishop did, and he sent his apologies and understood when Raheem no longer wanted to be involved in the drug world, which was funny because originally, he didn't even want to be in the business world, and now he was thriving. We all were.

Life had a funny way of doing things, and it was crazy how all of this started from Goldie's lie. I still had my days occasionally where I would think about her and either smile or cry. I just never really knew which one it would be. I never blamed her for anything, because unlike me at that time, she was only trying to survive. But if she could see me now, I knew she would be so turnt up and happy for me. She would live on in my heart. I ended up going back to South Carolina last year to visit her grave, and I sat out there until the sun went down because I knew once I left, I was never going back. I didn't run into anyone I knew, because I didn't stay in the state for longer than a day. And while I was there, I rode by my mama's house and saw her outside and a different last name on our mailbox with some young kids who looked exactly like me. So I assumed she got married, had kids, and moved on with her life without me, and that was okay because I'd done the same and accepted that everything couldn't always be mended.

"Munch, you okay?" Jody questioned, and I nodded.

"Yes. I couldn't be better. But I think I'm going outside to hit the blunt right fast before these kids really get active," I said, standing up.

"Oh, you so fake!" she yelled at me.

"I love you too, boo. I'll be back," I said and then walked outside after she tossed a pillow at my back.

"What's up, baby?" Raheem asked, holding his hand out so I'd come sit in his lap.

"Nothing much." I walked over to him and took a seat, and he wrapped his arm around me and rested his hand on my thigh.

"This a dry ass housewarming. Where er'body else at?" Stunna asked, smirking at us.

"I'm so sick of this, nigga." Raheem laughed and started choking on the blunt. "Fuck you. You know we don't got no damn friends but y'all."

"And after that shit with Dula, I'll never trust another female again other than Jody. Nope. I'm good off that." I shook my head.

"True. True. That hoe got on some Lifetime Movie Network type shit, ain't it? How much time she ended up getting for what she did anyway?" Stunna asked, looking over at me.

"Twenty-five damn years. Bitch should've got life." I sucked my teeth.

"It's all good. We got our son, and we got our daughter. We getting married, and I'ma put some more babies in you. Life is good. Please don't hold on to that shit, because after the way karma busted us upside the motherfucking heads, I don't even wanna think no negative shit!" Raheem yelled.

"Big facts! Let me go check on my wife," Stunna said, hopping up like he'd been away from Jody for an hour, but I loved the way he loved her.

"Munchie," Raheem said as I gave him the blunt back. I only needed to hit it a couple of times to get right.

"Yes?" I asked softly.

"I love you so damn much."

"I love you even more, Rah." I turned and kissed him as Stunna came back to the patio door.

"Y'all get y'all ass in here. We need to make a toast or sumthin'. This shit dry." Stunna carried on, and we laughed as we got up, and Raheem put the last bit of the blunt out.

"Take yo' ass to da ocean, then nigga. We on some chill shit these days," Rah joked as we went inside. The kids were still running around and playing, and it warmed my heart to watch them.

"Jo Jo, you want some grape juice for the toast?" I asked ,and she rolled her eyes playfully.

"What else I'ma drink, Munchie?" she asked, and I grinned as I walked in the kitchen to fix our drinks.

Once I had them, I brought them in the living room and gave everyone a glass. Unlike the last toast I'd had, this one actually meant something.

"To the newly engaged couple. I wish y'all many blessings and happiness, my sister and brother. Y'all deserve it as much as anyone else, and as long as you've learned from your past decisions, that's all that matters. Stay up," Stunna said, raising his glass, and everyone raised theirs before taking a sip.

The moral of the story was, if you were going to ride for someone, you'd better make sure they were riding for you. *Cheers.*

THE END

STAY CONNECTED WITH DEJAH RICE:

Author Page: https://www.facebook.com/Authoress.DejahRice
Facebook: https://www.facebook.com/kadejah.rice
Reader's Group: https://www.facebook.com/
groups/319584375229056
Instagram: Dejah_Rice_
Email: KadejahRice@gmail.com

ALSO BY DEJAH RICE

Made in the USA
Las Vegas, NV
04 November 2023